HEAD-ON!

A third shot, with a heavier note, boomed out, and the lane was suddenly full of echoes and swearing and the sounds of running feet. Too tall to be Moody, too slight for Meredith. I stepped out and tried to raise my gun, but he arrived too soon. Too soon for him as well. He swung something short and stubby at me; I ducked under the swing and dived forward, hitting about knee high and sending him thumping hard onto the ground, headfirst. There was a roar as the shotgun he had been carrying hit the brick wall and went off. Pellets flicked around, ricocheting from the bricks and roadway. . . .

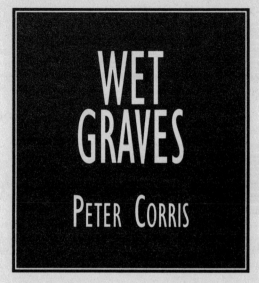

WET GRAVES

Peter Corris

A DELL BOOK

Published by
Dell Publishing
a division of
Bantam Doubleday Dell Publishing Group, Inc.
1540 Broadway
New York, New York 10036

First published in Australia and New Zealand in 1991 by Bantam

ISBN: 0-440-21750-4

Reprinted by arrangement with Transworld Publishers Pty Limited

Printed in the United States of America

Published simultaneously in Canada

August 1995

10 9 8 7 6 5 4 3 2 1

OPM

For
Rodney Booth, Sue Cummings,
and the flathead

For specialist information on body disposal, recovery, and pathology, my thanks to John Carmody, Paul Rosswood, and Lyndsay Brown.

PART
ONE

1

I'D BROUGHT THE LETTERS FROM MY HOUSE IN GLEBE TO MY DARLINGHURST OFFICE to give myself something official-feeling to do there. The Bankcard account and the electricity bill had gone up on the notice board to wait until I had the money and the inclination to pay them, but the two other envelopes looked more interesting. They were long and made of heavy-duty paper, the kind you slit open rather than rip apart with your fingers. Both carried Sydney GPO box numbers to which they should be sent if wrongly delivered, but they had got their man: Mr. Clifford A. Hardy. I took a Swiss army knife out of a drawer in the desk and slitted.

The first letter was from the office of the sheriff of New South Wales informing me that my number had come up. I was a citizen, a ratepayer, a voter and eligible for jury duty. Unless I was disqualified for some reason, I was obliged to fill out the attached form and hold myself ready to serve as a good man and true. I'd met the requirement for going on twenty-five years and had never been invited before. I felt rather pleased about it—responsible, mature, a serious person with a stake in the community.

The other letter was from a Detective Sergeant Lawrence Griffin of the commercial licensing division of the New South Wales police, requiring me to present myself in one week's time before the Glebe local court sitting as a court of petty sessions, to show why my private enquiry agent's license should not be canceled and why I "should not be disqualified either permanently or temporarily from holding a license." I'd been a private detective for a shorter time than I'd been a solid citizen, but long enough. I thought I was in good standing. I'd had my license threatened by the odd cop before, but that was usually heat-of-the-moment stuff—when someone was angry because of something I'd done or said. More often said. But never anything as heavy as this. How could a man fit to serve on a jury not be fit to hold a PEA license? It was bureaucracy run mad.

"This is unfair," I said to the old army surplus filing cabinet in the corner of the room. "There's no justice."

The filing cabinet didn't say anything, but as

I addressed it, I remembered that I had a copy of the Commercial Agents and Private Enquiry Agents Act of 1963 somewhere inside it. So perhaps it was talking to me. Sometimes I think I'm becoming more of a mystic as I get older. I put this to my friend Harry Tickener in the bar of the Journalists' Club recently, and he said it was just age and loneliness. "Get a girlfriend," Harry said, "get a tenant."

"I've had both," I said. "They—"

"Don't last. I know. Have another drink. I'd sooner see you drunk than mystical."

Certainly I'd ended up more drunk than mystical that night and a good few other nights lately. "Time to open new files," I said to the cabinet, "new windows on the world." I remembered that there was a bottle of red wine in the cabinet as well as the Commercial Agents and Private Enquiry Agents Act of 1963, the instrument that ruled my life. I got up to commune with both. The office was gloomy, but it was bright outside; an open window would be a good idea, too. I was half-way across the room when a firm knock came on the door. I turned, took two steps, and opened the door. "Come in," I said.

The woman who stood in the doorway was close to six feet tall and strongly built. She wore a tailored blue smock with a red sweater underneath it and shoes with low heels. Her face would have been described in some quarters as "weather-beaten." In fact, she had good features, thick dark hair with some gray in it, and if her brown skin had a few more lines and grooves in it than *Vogue* recommends, bad luck for *Vogue*.

"You couldn't have made it from the desk to the door in that time," she said. "Not possible."

"No. You're right. I was heading for the filing cabinet when you knocked."

"Do it then," she said. "I believe in finishing what you start."

"Mmm." I agreed with her, of course. Tried to do just that, but momentarily I'd forgotten what I wanted from the cabinet. Couldn't let that show. I waved at the client's chair, shuffled forward, and reached for the handle of the top drawer. "Please take a seat."

She strode across the frayed carpet as if she were used to rough ground and lowered herself into the chair. Memory returned when I saw the yellowed edges of the foolscap folders in the drawer and I rummaged through looking for my copy of the act of the Parliament of New South Wales. I found it in the second drawer, a bit dog-eared from being pushed aside rather than from assiduous reading. I pulled it out and slammed the drawer shut. She didn't react. *Good nerves or very preoccupied,* I thought. I flipped the slim document onto the desk, sat down, and tidied the papers in front of me.

"How can I help you?" I said.

She leaned forward and placed on the desk the card on which my name and the words *Private Enquiries* were written. There was a hole

in the card where the drawing pin that held it
to the door had been. "This was on the floor,"
she said.

"Thank you."

"Careless, but you don't go in for waste. I
like that."

I felt I was holding ground, just. "Good." I
pulled a notepad toward me and clicked a
Biro. "I'm supposed to keep notes on everything I do. Even if we don't do any business. I
usually start by asking for a name."

She smiled, and the lines around her eyes
spread. "I suppose if you can't even get a
name, there's not much likelihood of doing
business. I'm Louise Madden. I want you to
find my father, Brian Madden. He went missing two months ago. You can write that
down."

I did. "My fees are a hundred and eighty
dollars a day plus expenses," I said.

She nodded. "You seem rather . . . formal.
I didn't expect that. I've had enough of formality. I was hoping for some energy."

"I can usually guarantee that." I straightened the two letters and held them up. "I've
been hit with a bit of formality myself lately. It
must've rubbed off. I think I can promise you
professionalism and independence." I felt
stuffy and middle-aged as I spoke. I'd given up
smoking years ago, and the bottle of wine was
still in the cabinet, so there were no careless,
youthful gestures to be made. I underlined her
name on my notepad.

"I landscaped a garden for Roberta Landy-Drake," Louise Madden said. "A former client of yours. She recommended you."

That was good news. Mrs. Landy-Drake expected a good job and paid handsomely for it. She held the view, unusual for a rich person, that the laborer was worthy of his hire. "That's a good recommendation for us both," I said.

"Yes, she's fun, isn't she?"

This woman was full of surprises. People don't usually talk about fun in the same breaths as their dead dads. Still, attitudes to dead dads differ. I nodded and wrote "Landy-Drake" on my pad. Then I gave Ms. Madden my level, professional stare, the look that's supposed to get them talking.

"My father was last seen in May. He was walking across the harbor bridge."

"Why?"

"He liked to walk. He walked everywhere. It was recreation and exercise for him. No one seems to have understood that."

"By no one, you mean . . ."

"The police. The missing persons branch, or whatever it is. They haven't been helpful. They don't seem interested. They don't say so, but I have the feeling they think he jumped, committed suicide, not that they use the word."

"They try to avoid calling deaths suicides. They say it's to spare the feelings of the family."

"I'm his only family. It didn't spare my feelings. Is there another reason for avoiding the word?"

"Doesn't look good in the state statistics. Bad for business, bad for tourism."

"Christ. The hypocrisy," she said.

The real feelings were starting to seep out now under the layer of toughness. She wasn't about to pull out tissues and weep, but the emotions were working inside her.

At this point in an interview, there're two ways to go: operate on the emotions, get yourself a case and most likely a lot of confusion and trouble, or try to steady things down and see if there's really a job of work to be done. I've gone both ways in my time, but I'm a little too old now for confusion, so I went the other way. "I've had a lot of dealings with the police over missing persons reports. Their procedures can be puzzling to laypeople, Ms. Madden," I said. "Efficiency can look like indifference. If there's anything I can clarify for you, I'll—"

"Don't patronize me, Mr. Hardy. I don't need anything clarified, thank you very much. My father did not commit suicide. Will you help me find out where he is or what's happened to him?"

"Have you got anything to support your opinion that he didn't kill himself?"

She nodded vigorously. "I knew the man. He was a happy, easygoing man, in good health, with no problems of any kind. He wasn't bored. He loved life."

9

"Maybe the police mentioned misadventure? Misadventure strictly means accident."

"Some accident. Have you walked across the bridge lately?"

I hadn't, but from driving across it more times than I cared to remember, given the toll, I had an impression of a high fence beside the footway. I found myself drawing a rough sketch of the coat hanger, complete with cross-hatching and the water underneath.

Louise Madden drew a deep breath. "I don't expect miracles. Roberta said you have friends in the police force. Can you talk to them, find out what they did, and see if there's any more to be done? They *must* have been left with questions."

"I don't want to sound reluctant to work for you, Ms. Madden, but I like to have everything understood up front. Private inquiries can be expensive and inconclusive. They've passed a freedom of information act in this state against all my expectations. You could apply for all documents and material considered by the police. That might be all I get, anyway."

"No! It'd take months or years. This thing is eating me up. I'm trying not to let it obsess me, trying to keep a sane perspective on things."

"I'd say you were doing fine."

"Thank you. But I want something done—now!"

"Okay. I'll get the details from you—names, dates, and so on—and I'll need a retainer of a thousand dollars. Any unexpended part of that's refundable."

"Good." She got a checkbook from a pocket in her smock, and I started asking questions and writing down answers. Louise Madden was thirty-five, single, no children, self-employed. She had a degree in agricultural science from the Hawkesbury College, and she lived at Leura in the Blue Mountains. Her landscape gardening business employed three people beside herself and was prospering. Her father, Brian Madden, fifty-six, schoolteacher, of flat 3, 27 Loch Street, Milson's Point, had been reported missing early on the morning of May 5. A man answering his description had been seen walking toward the bridge footway from the north shortly after dawn. I got the names of the police officers Ms. Madden had spoken to in person and on the telephone. She'd kept notes of the conversations and was prepared to let me see them.

"Have you got a key to his flat?"

"No. There was no need. Dad always leaves a key under a flowerpot at the back."

"Trusting," I said.

She passed her check across the desk. "He's a lovely man, Mr. Hardy. He's gentle and kind. My mother died when I was twelve. Lots of fathers couldn't have coped, but my dad did. I never felt that I lacked for anything, not really."

"No money worries?" I said.

"My mother had had a long and expensive

illness, and I think Dad was still paying off hospitals and doctors for years after she died. He loved the school he was at and wouldn't go for promotions that'd take him away. So there wasn't much money, but it never seemed to matter. I went to James Ruse High and on from there. It must have been tough for him at times, but he never complained."

"You say his health was good?"

She tucked the checkbook away, clicked off her pen, and gave me *her* level look. "You mean, what about his sex life? You'd probably also like to know about mine. Mmm?"

"Natural curiosity, nothing more."

She grinned. "Dad played golf at Chatswood. I understand there was a woman there he spent some time with. I don't know her name, but I could find out. We saw each other most weeks, Dad and me, but we didn't live in each other's pockets."

"The name could be useful."

"You're being diplomatic, I see. I'm bisexual, and I'm between partners at the moment. I believe in being up front, too, Mr. Hardy, and I want you to understand that I owe my dad more than he's got from the bloody police so far."

"I understand. I'll do everything I can. Have you got a recent photograph of your father?"

"Not very recent. The one I had I gave to the police, and they haven't returned it yet."

"I should be able to get hold of it."

She stood up and straightened her smock. "I must say I'm a bit disappointed."

"How's that?"

"Roberta said you were . . . charming and quite funny."

I was standing, too, by this time, and I waved my hand at the papers on the desk. "I've got a few problems that're cutting down on the charm and the laughs. Tell you what, though, I could show you something that'd give you a laugh."

"What's that?"

"My garden. The only way to landscape it'd be with a jackhammer."

So at least I sent her off smiling.

I took a fresh manila folder, wrote "Madden" on the outside, tore off the three sheets of notepad, and put them inside. Begin as you mean to go on—neat and tidy. Then I leafed through the forty-five printed pages of the act. As I read, the lines from the Paul Simon song came into my head: "There must be fifty ways to leave your lover." There were nearly that number of ways to lose your license, temporarily or permanently: To commit an indictable offense was a pretty good way, also to be cited adversely in evidence given in court; to employ as a subagent an unqualified person could get you in trouble; and "unduly harassing any person" was pretty bad. A bit farther down in section 17, subsection 1, I found it: "Every licensed private enquiry agent shall paint or affix and keep painted or affixed on his place of business in a conspicuous position a notice showing in legible characters his name and description as a licensed private enquiry agent."

The damning evidence was right there on the desk in front of me—the card with the hole through it. I didn't even have the pin. I was in total breach of 17(1). But how could they know? The card had been on my door when I came in an hour before, hadn't it? Well, had it? I couldn't be sure.

All good clean fun, but it wasn't funny, really. The license was my meal ticket. Without it, I couldn't earn Ms. Madden's thousand bucks or anyone else's. I had a mortgage to pay and a Ford Falcon to support. I had bills on the notice board at home, and I needed about two thousand calories a day to keep going. I folded the letter and put it in the pocket of my sports jacket, which hung on the back of the chair I sat on. No doubt about it, I was neat and tidy today. I could drop in on my mate Detective Inspector Frank Parker and get a look at the missing persons file on Brian Madden and talk over the Hardy license-lifting case at the same time. Maybe I'd meet a nice, friendly woman at police headquarters and bump into someone at the bottle shop who was looking for a clean, light room in Glebe: eighty dollars a week, share the bills, and feed the cat.

I got up and put on my jacket. Then I saw the jury duty notice and bent over to fill in the form attached. I ran my eye down the fine print and discovered that licensed enquiry agents were ineligible to serve on juries. I crumpled the letter and scored a direct hit on the wastepaper basket.

2

THE LETTER FROM DETECTIVE SERGEANT GRIFFIN HAD INVITED ME TO CONTACT HIS office for more information about my court appearance, but I had something of Ms. Madden's caution about writers of official letters. "Bypass a bureaucrat today" is my motto. There ought to be a T-shirt.

I set out to walk to the new police fortress in Goulburn Street, partly for the exercise and partly because I like to see how my law-and-order tax dollar is being spent. I went down William Street and cut up Yurong to Oxford. It was July but warm and dry after a few weeks of cold and wet, and the lightly dressed and briskly moving people seemed to be relishing the change. These days I feel like closing my eyes when I walk through the city. You can't rely on a building you visited on Friday afternoon still being there on Monday morning, and most of the new stuff going up looks as if it has been designed by architects who stalled at cubism.

As I turned out of Oxford Street, I almost collided with a man who was so wide he almost took up half of the footpath. If the woman standing behind him had been at his side, they would have had to erect a detour sign.

"Say, buddy. Can you direct us to your Sydney Harbour Bridge?"

I pointed and tried to use language they would understand. "Walk north," I said. "It's a mile or so."

His mouth dropped open, and the fat on his cheeks sagged toward his neck. "Walk? Did you hear that, honey? We have to walk."

The woman, wearing a white sweatshirt and black trousers, looked like a two-tone bowling ball. "Isn't there a bus or a streetcar?"

I shook my head. "Better to walk. The buses are full of muggers." I nodded, stepped onto the road to get around them, and headed toward the police building. I regretted being a smart-arse before I got there and turned around to make amends, but they were getting into a cab, him in front, her in the back. I made a mental note to be nice to the next tourist I met.

From a distance the Sydney Police Centre looks all right—a combination of gray shapes, more or less inoffensive. Up close the slim pillars and the boxy structures behind them look like a house of cards propped up by king-size cigarettes. The architects have inserted grass and bricks everywhere grass and bricks can go and haven't stinted on polished marble and automatic doors. I went into the lobby, which looks like a cross between a bank, heavy on the bulletproof glass, and a five-star hotel, heavy on the pile carpet and rounded edges. The place bristles with pamphlets emphasizing community policing, and the lighting is soft to suggest that harmony and understanding begin here. The only thing to suggest that crime is being fought here, too, is that the cops in the glass and aluminum bunkers wear their caps.

I presented my credentials to a series of interceptors who made phone calls and ran metal detectors over me. A young constable escorted me silently up two flights of stairs and along a corridor to Frank Parker's office. We stood outside the door, and I looked at the cop.

"Am I allowed to knock or do you have to do it?"

"You can knock, sir."

"Thank you."

I knocked and I heard Frank say, "Yes."

"What now?"

The constable opened the door. "Mr. Hardy to see you, sir."

"Thanks, son. Come in, Cliff."

My escort had snapped back into a position resembling attention. I said, "At ease," and went into the room. The door was closed quietly behind me.

"Take a seat, Cliff," Frank said. "What's the matter with you? Why are you looking like that?"

"I've been a prick to people twice in the last twenty minutes," I said. "I don't know what's wrong with me." I sat in one of the two well-padded chairs and looked around the room. Frank's office in the old College Street police building had looked something like a World War I trench and smelled like a snooker hall. This was all beige carpet, off-white walls, and tinted glass. The old fixed squads in the police force—homicide, vice, fraud, and so on—had been broken up in favor of units that drew on personnel as required and pursued cases as directed by policy makers who weren't always policemen. Unlike the old top cops, who had diplomas from rugby league clubs and testimonials from priests and master masons, these guys had L.L.B.'s and criminology degrees and used terms like *targeting* and *social worth*. Frank's job was to liaise between the thinkers and the doers, so he got carpet and tinted glass. He liked the new honesty but missed the old sweat and dirt.

"Can't afford a conscience in your game, Cliff," Frank said. "Maybe you can do a few good deeds and get even. Meantime, I hate to push you out of the confessional, but . . ." He gestured at his thick stratifications of paper-work.

"I thought we might go out for a beer."

"No chance. I've got a meeting in fifteen minutes."

Frank looked grayer of hair and skin than he used to, but maybe it was the tinted glass. Then again, we hadn't played tennis in months or sat in a beer garden, so I suspected lack of sun was the cause. His nose was dipping toward his papers. Not the time to encourage him to take more exercise. I put my two requests to him, and he had the phone off the hook before I finished talking. He read while he listened, grunted, and made notes through the two calls. He put the phone down and looked at his watch. I can take a hint; I stood and moved toward the door.

"Hold on, Cliff. Let me think. Yeah, I reckon I can do it. What about a beer around about six tonight?"

"I thought you didn't have time to drink beer. I got the feeling that if you *did* drink beer, you wouldn't have time for a piss afterward."

"Don't joke. This could be serious. You've been mentioned in evidence given in the Lenko trial."

"What?"

"That's what Griffin tells me."

Beni Lenko was an alleged hit man accused of shooting and killing the husband of Didi Steller. Didi was a society woman with much more money than sense who'd ordered the hit on her hubby and then taken a kilo of sleeping pills. Beni complained about being short-changed on his fee and had talked his way into a murder charge. I'd read about the case in the papers, but to the best of my knowledge, I'd never met Didi, Beni, or the late husband, whatever his name had been. I stood on Frank's beige carpet with my mouth hanging open. "That's crazy," I said.

"I'll try to find out more about it and fill you in at six. Meantime, you'd better get on to Cy Sackville."

"I will. Thanks, Frank. I don't understand this." An indifferent day had got worse, much worse, but I wasn't going to drop my bundle. Not Hardy. "What about the Madden matter?"

"You can collect a copy of the file and a few other bits and pieces from room ten, second floor." Parker scribbled on a sheet of notepaper, came out from behind his desk, and handed it to me. He straightened his tie and worked his shoulders inside his well-tailored suit jacket. "Give them this. Sorry, Cliff, I really have to go. Six tonight at the Brighton?"

"Sure. Have a good meeting." I went out of the room and was picked up by another fresh-faced constable at the end of the corridor and escorted to level 2, room 10. I handed in the chit Frank had given me and was directed to wait downstairs. The waiting room didn't contain any magazines or ashtrays; they don't really want anyone to wait there for very long.

Like the man and woman already there, I sat on a hard chair and stared at nothing. I didn't know about them, but I had plenty to think about. I'd read about the Lenko trial and heard radio reports, but the details weren't clear in my mind. Had there been a mistrial or was an appeal pending? I couldn't remember.

I was getting more edgy by the minute. Having your license lifted is no picnic. The procedures were swift, bordering on brutal. The wording of the act had stuck in my mind. If you were disqualified at the court of petty sessions, you could appeal, but "Every such appeal shall be in the nature of a rehearing and the decision of the district court thereon shall be final and without appeal." Not even Cy Sackville could draw that out very far. There probably were procedures for reinstatement, but they were bound to be long and expensive.

In short, this was real trouble, and I was on the point of getting up and phoning Sackville when my name was called. I almost didn't answer. *You don't have time to investigate a bridge jumper*, I thought. *Your survival comes first.* But I told myself the Lenko business was all a mistake anyway. *Frank'll probably have it sorted out by six. Who could resist a man from such an office wearing such a suit?* I went to the desk and collected a large manila envelope from the female constable whose blond hair flowed out becomingly from under her hat. She advised me to have a nice day.

"You, too," I said. My positive attitude was working; I was being nicer to people. But just to show I wasn't going soft, I got moving before an escort could be appointed and made a judicious selection of pamphlets in the lobby; they'd add a nice touch to my waiting room if I ever got one.

It was close to three o'clock and I hadn't had any lunch. Lately I'd been trying to make lunch an exception rather than a rule. Another rule was no drinking before six. Well, as the sportsmen say, you win some and you lose some. I walked up Riley Street, and instead of dodging through the traffic, I used the crossing to get over to the Brighton Hotel; all that community policing soft sell was having an effect. I bought a seven-ounce glass of red wine at the bar and obeyed the notice there by "stepping back once served." Besides, stepping back helped me ignore the big, fat plastic-wrapped salad sandwiches that sat beckoningly on the bar.

The pub was quiet. Cops drink there, and journalists and punters and secondhand dealers; but everyone over twenty is drinking less these days, and the Brighton doesn't have slot machines and keeps the television turned down. My kind of place. I got a stool and a bit of shelf by the window where there was enough light to read by and ripped open the envelope. Inside was the sort of stuff Louise Madden would probably have been able to get under the freedom of information legislation if she'd been prepared to wait until she turned forty.

The photostat of the form Ms. Madden had filled in when making her report didn't tell me anything new. The notes of several police officers who'd made inquiries had been entered on a computer by a poor speller with an imperfect grasp of the computer's working. Added to that, the dot matrix printer which had spewed out the papers had had a faded ribbon. It all made for difficult and uninspiring reading. Madden's colleagues at the school had nothing useful to say; likewise his neighbors, doctor, and bank manager. The man had disappeared. If he'd been beamed up into a spaceship, the aliens were looking at a fifty-six-year-old male Caucasian *Homo sapiens*, six feet tall, weighing 155 pounds, with salt-and-pepper hair, blue eyes behind spectacles, and wearing a red tracksuit with white Nike running shoes. He spoke French and German pretty well, was widely read in history, anthropology, and golf. A valuable catch.

I reproached myself for taking things too lightly. Maybe it was the rough red on an empty stomach, but it was more likely to be the effect of the face in the gray, grainy photostat copy of the photograph Louise Madden had supplied. A kind, gentle man, she'd said. He looked it, as well as humorous, slightly mocking, and good-natured. More often than not the picture you get of the subject in a missing persons case is of a sullen-looking teenager or an adult with a distracted, self-absorbed look that indicates something deeply wrong and makes disappearance seem almost the right answer. Not so with Brian Madden. He looked like a nice man to know, fun to be with, and I wanted to find him.

I riffled through the notes and located a brief record of interview with one Peter Thornybush, who was a member of the foursome Madden used to play with at Chatswood. The others were Clive Wells and Carlo Calvino, schoolteacher, accountant, and lawyer respectively. Thornybush couldn't account for Madden's disappearance and ventured the opinion that Wells and Calvino were similarly ignorant. The police hadn't interviewed the other two, nor was there any trace of an interview with a woman connected with the golf course. House calls, possible leads—the weft and warp of the private detective's business. Another thread to pull was the taxi driver who'd seen a man answering Madden's description approaching the harbor bridge.

I finished the glass of wine, put the papers back in the envelope, and stuffed the police pamphlets in with them. I had two choices: to sit there drinking and worrying about the threat to my livelihood, or to get out there and do some work. It was four o'clock, and there was a good chance that someone I knew would

wander in any minute and affect my decision.
I got off the stool and left the pub, striking a
blow for self-direction. I even knew where I
was going.

3

WALKING ACROSS THE HARBOR BRIDGE NOWADAYS MUST BE ABOUT AS RISKY AS STREET marching in Beijing. The approaches—narrow paths, slender traffic islands, high-speed zones —were not pedestrian-friendly. Still, there were people, dwarfed by the huge gray metal superstructure and the big sandstone towers, walking across on both sides of the bridge. I drove. Trains rumbled past at twice the speed of the road traffic; only the motorcyclists, weaving between the cars, gave them any competition. I saw a jogger stop, pull off his Walkman headphones, and tap the mechanism. All that metal must play hell with the radio reception.

I drove across from the south side, necessarily slowly on account of the evening rush, turned in North Sydney, and crawled back. I hadn't asked which side of the road the person who might have been Brian Madden had been walking, but it didn't matter much. The footpath on the west side was crammed between the train tracks and a eight-foot-high fence. Same sort of fence on the east—solid metal to waist height, then cyclone wire stretched between uprights that curved over away from the gap for the last four inches or so. Three strands of barbed wire on top. A reasonably active person could climb it, and a strong man could get a 155-pound weight over it, but there the possibilities ended. Anyone going over that fence either wanted to or went because someone else wanted him to.

The sun was going down as I stop-started along in the lane for drivers who didn't have the right money to pay the toll. The sky was clear, and the water turned red-gold. The ferries and sailing ships seemed to be skating across a sheet of beaten bronze. I was buying fifteen minutes of a $100-million view for $1.50—a bargain. I found it strangely disconcerting to think of the work going on to tunnel under the harbor. It seemed wrong somehow, a violation.

The city skyline was impressive: irregular and cranky-looking, the way a skyline should be. A good many of the tall buildings were owned by insurance companies and housed insurance officers. They were the sorts of places I might have ended up in if I'd stayed in the insurance game. Even being stuck in the harbor bridge traffic was better than that. I turned on the radio to listen to the *Law Report* and got quite involved in a discussion on the niceties of defamation, remembering something about it from long ago. Before I was an insurance investigator, I had been a soldier and before that a law student. Life's twists and turns. I paid my toll and threaded my way back through the city streets to Darlinghurst. Lawyer A said that the defamation laws were fine as they were; lawyer B said they should be changed to enhance the public's right to know; lawyer C said they should be tightened to protect privacy. They were very polite to one another and seemed to disappoint the program's presenter.

Frank was waiting for me in the hotel with a half-drunk light beer in front of him and a worried look on his face. The bar has a door onto Riley Street and one onto Oxford Street, and there seemed to be more people coming in through both doors than going out. Frank had reserved me a stool with a folded copy of the evening paper and no doubt the frequent use of his tough-cop look. Frank had been a very tough cop when he was in homicide, and a very smart one. I wasn't sure just how tough he still was. I bought two middies of light and occupied the stool. The television was off, and the drinkers were talkers rather than shouters.

"So," I said.

Frank folded the newspaper and stuffed it in

the pocket of his jacket—okay in his homicide days, no way to treat the sort of suit he wore now. "Contacted Sackville yet?"

I drank some beer and shook my head.

"Don't take this lightly, Cliff. It's big trouble."

"I hoped you'd have it sorted out by this."

"Forget it." He leaned closer to me out of old habit, born of the days when he talked mostly to crims and fizgigs and other cops who liked to whisper. "A witness in the Lenko trial says you helped to set up the meeting between Didi Steller and Lenko, using Rhino Jackson as the go-between."

"That's crazy. Who is this witness?"

Frank took a sip of his beer. "When did you last see Jackson?"

The question surprised me, not because it was tricky in any way but because Frank was playing the copper rather than the friend. It was my turn to drink beer.

"Cliff?"

"I'm thinking. I'm wondering whether you really reckon I'd help to set up a hit or whether you're puzzling over who'd be trying to frame me."

Frank rubbed his chin, and the hard day-old bristles rasped like Scotch-Brite. "I'm sorry. All the crap I'm processing these days leaves me wondering if there's an honest man left in the world."

"Apart from yourself."

Frank took another drink and stared up

over my shoulder at the TV set, which showed film of some uniformed men using batons and fire hoses on young people wearing jeans and T-shirts. The street where this was happening looked hot and dusty; it could have been anywhere. "You know how they send the apprentice jockey for the left-handed whip, that sort of thing?"

I nodded.

"When I made it to plain clothes, they put me in vice. First job was go around the brothels picking up the take. Do it right, and get a good mark. Don't do it right, and your papers get marked 'Not suitable for plain clothes' and you can look forward to ten years in Woop Woop. Of course, once you've done it, the sergeant's got something on you, just as the senior sergeant's got something on him, and so on up."

"Nice. How did you handle that?"

"I found out what the senior had on the sergeant and used it against him to avoid the job. My papers got marked 'Not suited to this squad,' and I went over to homicide."

"They didn't get you to kill anyone?"

Frank grinned. "I was lucky I wasn't sent to armed holdup."

"This is fun, Frank," I said, "shooting the breeze. D'you want to talk about Hilde and my namesake next?" Hilde Stoner was a former tenant of mine who'd married Parker a few years back; they had a son named after me.

"No. Let's get back to it. The witness hasn't

got a name. She's in a witness protection program."

I looked at a clutch of men drinking at the bar—rebels who'd ignored the step-back order. "I don't understand what you're saying."

"All I can tell you now is that the witness is a woman. She made a very brief appearance in court during Lenko's first trial. I'm told she wore a wig and dark glasses; her own mother wouldn't have known her. Since then she's gone into witness protection, as I say."

"Why?"

"You haven't been keeping up, Cliff. A witness didn't show up, and couple of jurors were suborned, or attempts were made to suborn them. Threats, you know. So, mistrial, and Lenko goes up again in a couple of weeks."

"Who didn't show?"

"Rhino Jackson."

"Shit. Are you telling me you can't find out who this witness is?"

"No. I can find out, given time. But I'd be putting my job on the line if I told you. And I'm sure Sackville'd advise you not to see her. There's probably been an injunction issued to that effect anyway."

"Great. So I can't even know who's trying to put me out of business. Christ, Frank, this could lead to a conspiracy charge or something, couldn't it?"

"I said I'd help you. I—"

I took a drink of the light beer, wishing it were whiskey. "No. I'm not going to ask you to risk your job for me. You've got responsibilities. I haven't. I'll handle it somehow. You're right, I should've called Sackville the minute I got the letter. He must be able to throw a few punches for me."

"That's right. If he runs into trouble, tell him to call me. I'll do everything I can."

I thanked him, and we drank the rest of our beer. We did get around to talking a little about Hilde and the kid. I agreed to go out to Harbord and see them, and Frank agreed to play tennis soon. We both had our fingers crossed behind our backs. Frank told a few halfway funny stories about the politicians he came into contact with in his new job, and I told him about the client who'd hired me to guard his dog. It was a valuable dog.

The noise in the bar was mounting as the booze took effect. An argument was developing along from us; the voices were getting louder, and every second word was *fuck*. The cigarette fug builds up more slowly now that people have come to believe that smoking kills you, but it still builds. My eyes started to water, and Frank looked at his watch. He stood, took out his paper, rolled it, and tapped it against his open palm like a cop with a baton. His grin was pretty low-voltage. "You never answered my question, Cliff."

"What was that?"

"When did you last see Rhino Jackson?"

I was carrying my big manila envelope with the police documents and pamphlets inside. I held my paper shield up against his paper weapon. "Hell, Frank," I said, "you know I charge twenty thousand to set up a hit. And it's not easy. Who can protect that sort of money from the tax man these days?"

I didn't want to go home. The house is empty apart from the cat, and I don't even have Harry Soames next door to gripe about and with. I'm in number 57; Soames sold out in 59 to a developer, and the owners of 61 and 63 did the same. The word in the street is that a town house project is on the way, but the word doesn't explain why I haven't even been made an offer. I'd refuse it like I'd refuse the Order of Australia, but I wouldn't object to the offer. The cat would probably prefer to live in a town house.

I drove to St. Peter's Lane and parked in a place where my resident's sticker allowed me to stay as long as I liked. It had taken several visits to the South Sydney Council office, one to the Department of Motor Transport, two statutory declarations, and ten bucks to get the sticker, so I made as much use of it as I could. The area is changing, gentrifying fast. Primo Tomasetti's tattooing parlor has gone, along with the slab of concrete he used to rent me as a parking space. Blocked-off streets are making the place like a maze. I sometimes get the feeling that you can find your way around only in a BMW.

A wind had sprung up, and the mild day

had turned into a cold evening. The cold made me hungry. I bought a pizza in William Street and headed for my office, a smoke-free zone with weird but gentle neighbors like the painless depilator and the new iridologist; they wouldn't budge for developers without a fight. There was also the bottle of red in the filing cabinet to add to the allure. The threatened renovation of my building never happened— saved by the stock market crash. The lane has pretty much avoided gentrification; it still features more plastic garbage bags than native plants, and the occasional paint jobs the buildings get aren't modish. It's the church that saves us; if the God business goes any further downhill, we could be in big trouble.

One change we've had to endure is the installation of a lock on the street-level door. I keep my key to it wedged in a crevice of the church's sandstone wall on the other side of the lane. I keep a spare key to the office door under the lino on the stairs—a bit like in *Dial M for Murder*. You won't catch me locked out of building, office, and drinks cabinet on a cold Tuesday night.

I got the key out of the wall and had to juggle the pizza and my manila envelope of volunteered information to use it. I ended by wedging the envelope between my knees, balancing the pizza box on my head, and working the stiff key one-handed.

He came out of the shadows where there is a recess between my building and the next, and he was quiet and fast. I just caught a glimpse of him and swayed away a little from the thing in his hand that was swishing through the air. It struck hard, but the pizza saved me; it took a lot of weight out of the blow, although I felt it down to my toes and the shutters almost came up. I yelled and sagged back against the door. I felt a hand grabbing at me as if the assault were sexual, but I realized he was reaching for the envelope between my legs. I hunched over and attempted to butt him somewhere, anywhere. I connected and felt the wind rush out of him. It hurt me, too, forcing me to shut my eyes and gasp. I tried to yell again; but my windpipe felt twisted, and no sound came out.

I was going down, a perfect target for a boot, when a shout came from above and across the lane.

"Hey! What's going on there?"

The voice was coming from the church. Could it be the Almighty? I tried another yell but managed only a choked growl. Shout and growl were enough for my attacker. He stopped groping at me and ran off down the lane, stumbling a bit but with a lot more get-up-and-go in him than I had in me.

4

IN DARLINGHURST IF A SHOUT SAVES YOU FROM INJURY AND VIOLATION, YOU DON'T complain if you never see who did the shouting. I sat with my bum on the cold cement, my back against the door, and peered up at the high wall opposite. But there was no further movement or sound from that quarter. The envelope had slid to between my knees and was ripped where the attacker had got a grip on it, but that was all. My head was aching, ringing. I guessed the blurry white thing lying in the lane, upside down with a large dent in it, was my pizza box.

When I was sure I had vision and movement, I levered myself upright and looked around for my key. I couldn't see it on the ground. I picked up the pizza, squinted in the gloom and found the key in the lock. I opened the door and broke my fail-safe rule by putting the key in my pocket. The rule doesn't apply when you're semiconcussed and carrying a broken pizza. Then I went slowly up the stairs, pausing at each level, until I reached my own floor. I slid along the wall like a drunk needing the support until I reached my door. No need to dig for a key or, even worse, go back to the stairs for the one under the lino. The door was standing open.

I turned on the light, went inside, and put my burdens on the desk. I knew I'd left papers on the desk; my mother's attempts to make me tidy hadn't ever taken, and where she'd failed how could the army hope to succeed? But I hadn't left the desk as messy as this. I certainly hadn't ripped my copy of the Commercial Agents and Private Enquiry Agents Act of 1963 into pieces and scattered them around the room. I gave the door a push and heard it slap against the frame and fail to lock. The lock had been opened with a pick and had jammed in the latch position. That much detection was all I was up to for the moment. I went down the hall to the bathroom, ran water, washed my face, and got a thick wad of wet hand towel paper to press against the bump on my head.

I sat in the client's chair with my eyes closed for a while until the throbbing eased and other parts of my body made their needs known. I was hungry and thirsty. For no good reason I remembered something my ex-wife, Cyn, had said when I came home with a pizza one night. "Garbage in, garbage out," she'd said. That was all *she* knew; if I'd been carrying a tabouli salad, my brains might be lying in the lane. The filing cabinet had been opened—it didn't take Raffles to do that—but the wine was still there. I pulled the cork out of the bottle and drank some of the rough red down in gulps. Aggressive stuff, confidence-building. I slid the pizza out of the crushed box and wolfed it—cold, squashed anchovies and all. A few more gulps of wine, and I felt ready to plug in the jug and make coffee. Cyn had despised instant coffee, too, but even she couldn't deny that it was quick. Two cups of it, black, with three red Codrals, and I was pain-free, almost floating, ready to think about what the hell was happening to me.

The office had been roughly but thoroughly searched—filing cabinet, desk drawers, under the carpet, behind the electric jug, coffee, and sugar. For what? I did a quick paw-through myself and couldn't find anything missing, although I had a feeling that something was. The notes on my oldest case, the one involving the striptease dancer and her runaway son, and my latest, the disappearance of Brian Madden, were where they should have been. I prowled around the room trying to locate the gap. When things are too familiar, it's easy to overlook something missing; memory and imagination supply the lack. I drank some more wine and gnawed on a pizza crust.

What? What? Eventually it hit me. A framed photograph almost three decades old I had put in the office rather than the house because Cyn had hated it wasn't lying facedown on top of the filing cabinet the way it had for years. A clean space, 2⅓ inches by 4, stood out on the dusty surface like a cricket pitch on a bowling green.

I sat down behind the desk and thought about the picture. I'd looked at it a thousand times with mixed emotions, and every detail of it was clear in my mind. "Maroubra Police Boys' Club boxing championships" had been scratched across the bottom by the photographer. The picture showed the finalists in the divisions from heavyweight to flyweight—sixteen of us. I was there alongside Clem Carter, who'd knocked me out in the third round to win the welterweight title. Also in the picture were several policemen who'd trained and encouraged us and acted as timekeepers and referees. I'd long forgotten most of their names, but I remembered one of the referees. He'd tried to give me a fast count when I went down in the semifinal, and I'd had to scramble up early to beat it. You might think that a man who can't even referee a kids' boxing match honestly has a serious problem, and in this case you'd be right. His name was Stewart "Rhino" Jackson.

It didn't make a lot of sense, but it did make some. One thing was certain: It was time to get professional help on my semiprofessional problem. I poured a sipping-size measure of wine and called Cy Sackville. In an unguarded moment Sackville had once told me that he liked to watch *L.A. Law* on TV on Tuesday nights, so I knew where to find him. I dialed his number and tried to imagine him sitting in a leather armchair in his Point Piper flat with the remote control in one hand and the *Law Review Digest* in the other, ready to do a bit of reading during the commercials.

"Sackville. Please leave your message after the tone."

"I know you're there, Cy. Put in a tape, and press the record button. It's your old friend and client Cliff Hardy in need of a talk."

There was a pause. Then the tone was cut off, and Sackville's voice came on the line. "Jesus Christ! Hang on."

I grinned as I sipped the wine.

"Okay," Sackville said.

"How're Mickey and Grace? Are they married yet?"

"What d'you want, Cliff?"

"Ha, ha, can't say you're busy, can you?"

"I could hang up."

"Don't, Cy. I need help." I told him about the summons and Parker's sketchy information. I didn't tell him about the missing photograph or my sore head or the squashed pizza. Sackville's appetite for the law is insatiable. The best way to get his attention is to present him with some legal snafu he hasn't struck before. I get to do that reasonably often, and I could tell by his silence as I spoke that I'd hooked him with this one.

"Interesting," he said. "I've never been to one of these hearings."

"What hearings?"

"This petty sessions sitting you're going to. It's more in the nature of a hearing than a trial. Statements, right of reply, modified rules of evidence."

"I don't want to go to any hearing. I want you to get me out of it. It's bullshit. I wouldn't know Beni Lenko from Alan Bond."

"How about this Jackson?"

"I know him, sure. But there's no connection to the Steller-Lenko thing."

"How do you know? Have you looked into it?"

"Cy . . ."

"They must have something, Cliff. I know they're trying to tighten up on all you pistol-packing types—private eyes, security guards, and so on. Too many guns and payrolls going missing. But your nose is clean with the police, isn't it?"

"Yes."

"So there's someone behind it. I wouldn't press Parker on the name of the witness. These witness protection programs are the flavor of the month. A breach by Parker could seriously damage his career if it got known."

"I told him not to do anything to risk his job. But I can't just sit and wait for this shit to flop on me. They'd have to put you as my lawyer in the picture, wouldn't they?"

"Up to a point."

"What does that mean?"

"They needn't identify the witness specifically, but I would get a context—full transcript of statement, supporting evidence, and so on."

"Great. I can be put out of business by a faceless woman."

"Let me think," Sackville said.

"If you're sneaking a quick look at the box, Cy, I'll come around and piss in your pool."

"No, no. This is interesting. Don't worry, Cliff, I'm taking it seriously. What I'll do first off is get you a delay. I can probably get a fortnight, maybe more."

"What good will that do?"

"You're a detective, aren't you? You'd better ask around and find out who wants you retired. Are you vulnerable in any other way? What are you working on now?"

"A missing persons case."

"Sounds safe enough. Good, even. A little acceptable privatization of law and order. Keep your books in shape; account for your expenses. Write up your notes every day."

"My name card fell off the door."

"Get a proper plate made. Screw it to the door. You need to look solid."

Just hearing him say it made me feel all the

more fragile. He got the date of the hearing and had me spell the name at the foot of the fateful letter: G-r-i-f-f-i-n. He told me he'd get back to me when he had some news. I think he expected another crack about *L.A. Law*, but I disappointed him. My head was buzzing again, and the torn paper, turned-back carpet, and battered pizza box were depressing me. I added the documents I'd collected to the Madden file, put the police pamphlets on top of the filing cabinet, and gathered up my meager belongings. I freed the door lock, turned out the light, and left the office. I went down the stairs quietly and carefully, but no one was lurking in the shadows. So if my guardian angel was hovering around, he had nothing to do for the present. I stuck the key back in the wall, drove home, and went to bed.

In the morning, after eight hours' sleep, with only a slight headache and the cat for company, things seemed a lot clearer. I had a one-thousand-dollar fee to earn and a license to protect. "Keep busy, that's the secret" is what my Irish Gypsy grandmother used to say. She made it to eighty-plus and keeled over while putting up drywall. It was good advice, applicable to me at forty-plus, although the only physical labor I did these days was carrying out the garbage tin. As I told the cat, it was very simple. "Work on the Madden case in the daytime and the Lenko matter at night. Keep busy."

I washed a couple of days' worth of dishes and swept a fortnight's dirt from the floor. Then I shaved and stood under a shower, letting the warm water massage my bruised head. The bulldozers hadn't made their moves on the next two houses yet, and I was dreading the day. For the moment they stood empty, and my end of the street was unnaturally calm and peaceful. No Joni Mitchell from Soames, no revving Yamahas from number 63. I missed them both. The cat missed them more. Soames's cat was a wimpy part Persian that offered no competition to mine. The bikers—the house seemed to harbor a shifting population of leather-clad males and females—were an endless source of hamburger, pizza, and souvlakia scraps. The cat's calories were cut drastically when the places were sold. It drank its milk sullenly, curled up in a patch of sunlight, and was through for the day. "Have a good one, sport," I said.

I allowed myself a few minutes to sit in the sun and try to recall every nuance of the attack the night before. Nothing much came: male almost certainly, from an impression of size, and a smoker. No one who has given the habit up ever fails to detect the smell on hair and clothes. No Hercules—the blow hadn't been delivered with enormous power. But then, that might have been compassion. There'd been no sound, no speech. At a guess, a million or so citizens of the city could fill the bill.

I told myself this was a challenge. Keep

busy. By the time I was sitting in my car, turning the ignition key and putting on my sunglasses, I felt almost normal. If you can call a man who talks to cats normal.

5

I WAS DRIVING TO MILSON'S POINT TO SNIFF AROUND BRIAN MADDEN'S NEIGHBOR-
hood, get the feel of the man on his own terri-
tory, so I should have been thinking about
that. Madden in the daytime, Lenko at night.
Instead I found myself thinking about Rhino
Jackson. He'd be about ten years older than I
was, I reckoned, out of the police force for going on twenty years and into almost every
other related field of activity you could name:
security guard and courier, bodyguard, private
inquiries, security consultant for right-wing
political figures and organizations, and, I'd
often heard it rumored, part-time spook. I'd
run into him every few years or so in the
course of my work, and he always went out of
his way to be nice to me. He even apologized
once, when he was drunk, for the short count.

I'd forgotten about it until the apology reminded me. I found it impossible to like him
for no very good reason. Now I had a reason.

I took the first exit off the Bradfield Highway and cut back toward the water. I tried to
remember the last time I'd seen Jackson. It
had been a few years ago, not long after my
final break with Helen Broadway. I couldn't
remember anything about the meeting, except
that Jackson had been drunk. Maybe I'd been
drunk, too. Back then it wasn't too uncom-
mon. The thing about Jackson was that he was
good at what he did. He was an alcoholic, but
it never seemed to impair his functioning. He
changed course so often not because he was
incompetent but because he got restless. I'd
been told that or had worked it out for myself.
It seemed I knew more about him than I realized, but I didn't know why he was called
Rhino.

I waited at a red light behind a truck which
blocked out the water view I'd been looking
forward to, one of the rewards of driving
around Sydney. Indecision washed over me.
Which was more important: finding Brian
Madden or protecting my license? Also, which
was easier? I knew lots of places to look for
Rhino Jackson. The light changed, and I made
the decision to stick to the plan. *Tune out the
static, and put up the antenna,* I thought. *You
might get lucky and find Madden this morning.*

The truck turned left, and I got the view I'd
been waiting for. It's quite an eyeful—across

the sparkling water to the shining city. The water seems to sanitize things, to make it seem that a city blessed with such a setting couldn't possibly be a bad and dangerous place. We know better, of course; perhaps it's the tension between the appearance and the reality that makes the town exciting. I've said these things to people in loquacious moments, and a common reply has been "If you feel so hot for the water view, why haven't you got one?" That's a new Sydney sort of question. I give the old Sydney answer: "Because I like to look at it doesn't mean I want to buy it."

Milson's Point is bisected by the Bradfield Highway. Madden's flat was in the western sector at the high end of a short street with a view out over Lavender Bay. As in all older areas with a high proportion of flats, there wasn't much space to park in the street. The residents, who haven't got what the real estate agents call off-street parking, leave their cars at home and catch ferries and buses to work. They use their cars to go to shopping centers, beaches, and football grounds at the weekends. I got a space across the road and down the slope from number 27 and sat for a while to pick up the atmosphere of the street. Also, my head was still hurting and the view was restful. A few people came and went, mostly middle-aged or older. A motorcycle courier roared up, left his motor ticking, and ran across to a small block of flats. He scanned the letter boxes and went up a short flight of steps three at a time. He was back and performing a tight U-turn within a minute. I should have taken his registration number; the next time I needed to send something by courier I wanted him.

I locked the Falcon and strolled across the street. Number 27 was a white stucco building of somewhat unusual design. It housed three flats, on top of one another facing the street; another flat at the back ran at right angles to the others. This one was on two levels and rather bigger. On the lower level there were French doors opening onto a small garden. The effective entrance was on the upper level, reached by a set of iron steps. Good view of the water from here, sliver of bridge, slice of opera house. There was a small, tiled area at the top of the steps under a wooden pergola. Great place for breakfast: some weathered garden furniture, a few hardy vines in tubs, and one black plastic flowerpot. If you were hoping for a secreted door key, this was the place to look.

I bent, lifted the pot, and picked up the rusty key to flat 3. I knocked on the door and waited, as is only polite. Nothing. The key turned easily in the well-worn Yale lock, and I stepped into a short hallway that led to a series of smallish rooms which were dim because the blinds were drawn. The place had that closed-up, no-one-around-for-a-month smell that starts to soak into the carpets and curtains if it hangs about for much longer. I raised the blinds as I went quickly through the rooms, getting the feel of the place. There was a sitting room, a bedroom, and a bathroom upstairs; downstairs were the kitchen, a smaller bedroom, and a study. The flat was neat but not obsessively so. Books and magazines sat on shelves and surfaces without their edges lined up, a few clothes hung over chairs in the main bedroom, there were papers on the study desk, and rinsed but not washed dishes in the draining rack.

Normal, I said to myself, *very normal*.

On my second tour I paid more attention to detail: I examined the clothes, which tended toward the casual but included a couple of good-quality suits and an expensive overcoat; the books suggested an interest in modern political history and serious literature, with historical novels from a variety of periods thrown in for light relief. Madden's golf shoes were pricey but not new; likewise his clubs, which were stored in a cupboard under the stairs. There were a couple of bottles of wine in a rack, a half-empty bottle of Riesling and a couple of cans of beer in the fridge. I sat down at the study desk, opened the drawers, and went through his papers like an auditor. I found ample evidence of an orderly, bill-paying person. A taxpaying person with a superannuation scheme to guarantee him a comfortable but not riotous retirement. Madden kept his credit card slips for tax purposes, and there was too big a stack of them to go through in detail. A quick shuffle showed nothing out of the ordinary. There was a registration paper for a 1987 Ford Laser with an expiry date in February of the current year. No evidence of renewal. Madden had a checkbook and a savings passbook with unremarkable balances, deposits, and withdrawals. No diary, no medical bills out of the ordinary, no love letters or blackmail threats.

I found two photograph albums, neither very carefully kept or annotated. The pictures emphasized the normality and stability of Madden's life; there was a continuity to them, a continuity of people and places from young adulthood to middle age. The only interruption to the even flow was the absence from the snapshots, dating from about thirty years back, of the bright-eyed, dark-haired young woman who had been Brian Madden's wife. There were plenty of photographs of Louise, charting her growth from childhood to late teens. Only the odd picture from that point on. No shots from foreign holidays, no handsome schoolboys or young girls with old eyes.

A stack of letters lay on the living-room table. I surmised that Louise had collected them on an earlier, worried visit to the flat and that there would be more now in the letter box. I examined the letters but found nothing remarkable about them. The contents of most could be guessed from the envelopes: bills, subscriptions due, invitations, professional bumf. The telephone was on a shelf in the kitchen, stool beside it, pad for messages, address and telephone numbers book to hand. I'd recently met a young woman who didn't know the telephone number of her own flat, which she shared with a couple of friends. When I asked her how she rang home, she said, "I've got the number on autodial at the office. I don't *need* to know it." None of that nonsense for Brian Madden; his phone was the old dial-it-yourself model, and his address and numbers book was as old as the phone.

I raised all the blinds in the kitchen and sat down at the table to leaf through the book. Madden had printed the surnames and street names, but the numbers and first names were written in a hurried scrawl that probably came from taking lecture notes and marking essays. He seemed to know a lot of people and had recorded a good many institutional and business numbers, but not more than you'd expect for a well-educated man with broad interests: a theater booking agency, several restaurants and hotels, the state library and gallery, the ABC, David Jones, four taxi companies, two plumbers, an electrician, and so on. I recognized some of the personal entries: the journalist Max Walsh, the cartoonist Bruce Petty. Several of the names were crossed out, and since these included those of George Munster and Xavier Herbert, I concluded that these people were dead. I'm not big on intuition, let alone premonition, but I felt something not rational or logical at work as I looked at that entry—"X. Herbert, Red Lynch, Queensland, 4899," and the post office box number—with the firm lines passing through the letters, almost obliterating them. I sensed that Brian Madden was dead.

I put the address book down and went for another wander, in a somber mood now, alert to different things, through the flat. Most of the rooms carried a picture or two on the walls. A few originals by artists I didn't know; a couple of prints—a Roberts and a Streeton. Nice middle-of-the-road stuff. Over the small fireplace in the study there was a framed, enlarged-to-a-meter-square copy of the famous photograph that showed the two arches of the Sydney Harbour Bridge just before they were joined. The figures of workmen, right on top of the structure, stood out starkly against a light sky.

The morbid feeling stayed with me as I moved through the rooms. I was irritated with myself for giving way to it and tried to find something to give it rational support: pills, whiskey bottles, burned paper, a bloodstain. I found nothing. Feeling foolish, I examined the golf clubs, which told me nothing except that Madden apparently used the whole set, like someone who knew how to play the game. I upended the bag and only leaves, flakes of mud, and a couple of balls fell out. In one of the zippered pockets I found a batch of score cards. All but two of the cards were Madden's. He shot consistently in the eighties. One card had a jotting on it to the effect that Henry Bush owed Madden ten dollars after losing to him by three holes. The card was dated eighteen months back. Two of the cards were marked up in a different hand and carried the name Dell Burton. Madden and Dell Burton had played rounds together on April 1 and 25 at Chatswood. Madden had shot 86 to Burton's 87 on the first round; they'd both shot 88 on the second.

I found a telephone number and an address in Chatswood for Burton, D. in Madden's book. You didn't have to be Einstein to work out that Dell Burton was "the woman" Louise Madden had referred to. What else is there to do with "the woman"? I sat on the stool and dialed her number.

"Hello." Good voice, educated but not toffee. Mature-sounding.

"I'd like to speak to Dell Burton."

"Speaking. Who's this?"

"My name is Hardy, Ms. Burton. I'm a private detective. Louise Madden has hired me to investigate her father's disappearance."

"Brian's daughter? He said he'd never discussed me with her. I can't believe she gave you my number."

"No. She's aware of your existence, but nothing more. I'm calling from Mr. Madden's flat right now. I found a golf scorecard with your name on it and your number in his address book."

"I see. A private detective. Um, I don't know.

I've been calling Brian's number for weeks.
I've been to the flat. I thought about going to
the school, but—"

"I'd very much like to talk to you. Can I
come to Chatswood and see you? Is there a
problem in that?"

"What did you say your name was?"

"Hardy, Cliff Hardy. You can look me up in
the phone book, and you can call Louise Madden, if you want to check on me."

"I'll think about that. This *is* a little bit difficult, Mr. Hardy."

"Could we meet somewhere else?"

"I'm married. God, I've been so worried
about Brian! I can't understand what's happened. Is he—"

"I don't want to cause you any trouble, Mrs.
Burton. I just want to talk about Mr. Madden.
I need to understand him better if I'm to be of
any use. His daughter loves and admires him."

"So do I, Mr. Hardy."

"Good. Not many men have that much luck.
He must be a man worth knowing and worth
finding. I need to talk to you."

A pause while she digested that, and what
else? Does a Chatswood wife meet a man who
announces himself as a private detective over
the phone? On the other hand, can a woman
who has heard nothing from her lover in a
month afford not to meet someone who's apparently in the know?

"You wouldn't blame me for being cautious,
would you?" she asked.

"Not at all."

"Then I will look you up in the phone book, Mr. Hardy. Tell me, how did you get into Brian's flat?"

"His daughter told me where to find the key, under the flowerpot."

"I'll call the number in a few minutes." She hung up sharply.

Smart woman, I thought. *Taking precautions, keeping the initiative.* I flicked through the address book and located a name and number for Henry Bush. When the phone rang, I picked it up immediately and said, "Hardy."

"I'll meet you, Mr. Hardy. There's a coffee shop in Chatswood immediately across from the railway station. It's called the Chatterbox. Let's meet there in half an hour."

"Fine. How will I know you?"

I heard her sigh, and there was something like a catch in her voice when she next spoke. "Have you looked through Brian's things?"

"Some of them. I've been pretty thorough, I think."

"Have you seen a photograph of a golf foursome? Brian, a tall, bald man, and two women?"

"I think so."

"I'm the woman in the red sweater. The other man is my husband."

I thanked her, hung up, and went back into the study for the photograph albums. I had seen the photo but hadn't paid it much attention. A fine day on the golf course—ruddy cheeks, cotton shirts, windblown hair. Madden was standing next to a fair woman in a white jacket; they were watching the bald man demonstrating a shot to a woman who was frowning with concentration. She was small with a taut, energetic-looking body and cropped brown hair. Her red sweater was draped over her shoulders with the sleeves tied in front. She looked as if she couldn't wait to get hold of the club.

6

I PARKED IN ONE OF CHATSWOOD'S EXTENSIVE PARKING AREAS AND WALKED TOWARD the railway station. At a casual glance there wasn't much that I couldn't have bought in the shops, from a leather tie to a chocolate pavlova. On the other hand, I didn't see anything I actually needed. The Chatterbox was one of those bright, glossy places where everything was scrupulously clean, but you wouldn't put money on the chance of getting a good cup of coffee. I took a seat by the window and told the waitress that I was waiting for someone. She checked that the table, ashtray, and plastic-coated menu were spotless and went away. There were three or four other people in the café, all singles. No chattering just at present.

Dell Burton arrived five minutes after the

appointed time. She was wearing tight black trousers, the kind with a strap under the foot, high-heeled shoes, a loose blue sweater and helmetlike red felt hat. A leather bag like a small duffel was slung over her shoulder. She marched straight up to my table.

"Mr. Hardy?"

I lifted my bum off the chair. "Mrs. Burton."

We shook hands, and she sat down. She pulled off the hat and rubbed her hand over the cropped hair. All her movements were quick and busy. Her makeup was effective—a woman of about forty years of age looking her best. "Have you ordered?" she asked.

"Not yet." I looked up, and the waitress was there, magically ready.

"Long black for me," Mrs. Burton said.

"The same."

The waitress made two squiggles on her pad. "Anything to eat at all?"

We both shook our heads, and she left, gliding away over clean tiles in rubber-soled shoes. Mrs. Burton dug a crumpled soft pack of Marlboro out of her bag and offered it to me. I refused, and she lit up. "Three a day," she said. "Maybe four today, or ten. So?"

"I'm hoping you can tell me something about Brian Madden that'll help me to find him."

She blew smoke over my shoulder. "I wish I could. If I had any ideas, I'd have acted on them myself by now."

"Despite your . . . situation?"

"Yes. My situation, as you call it, is not all that tricky. My husband knows that I've been having an affair. He doesn't know with whom, and he doesn't want to know. They're the terms we struck. It works all right. I'm not housebound, no kids. I could've . . . looked . . ." She waved the hand with the cigarette in it, more emphatically than theatrically. "But I didn't know what I could do. I thought about trying to contact the daughter, going to his school. But . . ." The hand waved again, indicating lack of direction.

The waitress brought the coffee. I put a spoonful of raw granulated sugar in mine; she didn't take sugar, but she still stirred the cup with the spoon—the gesture of an ex–sugar user. She drew solidly on her Marlboro a couple of times and then stubbed it out. I waited for the waitress to spring up with a fresh ashtray, but a few new customers drifted in and took her attention. The coffee was a bit weak but acceptable. "Sane, balanced, contented people don't disappear for no reason," I said. "Either they fall victim to some random, senseless force or there's something in their lives, their backgrounds, that . . . removes them from the scene."

"You mean, makes them run away, change their names?"

I shrugged and drank some more coffee. "That sort of thing. You haven't tried your coffee. It's okay."

"I don't want it. I want another cigarette."

"Fight it."

"Know all about it, do you?"

"Not about moderation, just quitting."

She drank some of her coffee. "I couldn't, not possibly. Well, I hadn't ever thought about Brian in the way you say, about a random act or a reason for disappearing. I don't know what to think."

"You can't recall anything he said, or anything you overheard, or half heard, that suggested some problem in his life? Past or present. Some . . . disorder? What about his marriage? Any threads?"

"No. He spoke about his wife a few times, but there was nothing to suggest that it wasn't just a sad event in the past. Normal, almost."

I nodded. That was the word I had hit on when looking through the flat. "What about the daughter?"

Suspicion flared. She lowered her cup. "She hired you, you said."

"It's been known. You hire someone like me, but you don't give the real reasons."

Dell Burton shook her head. "Nothing. He's a nice, funny, warm man. Good in all sorts of ways. Good for me."

"You'll have to forgive me, Mrs. Burton. This is where it gets personal, and I have to be blunt. If you walk out, I won't try to stop you."

"You're softening me up in advance."

"Maybe. I can see that you're an intelligent, sophisticated woman. Perhaps a bit selfish."

"That's fair."

I put the coffee cup between her and the question. "Why didn't you leave your husband for Brian Madden?"

She lifted her cup. We were like two fencers, feinting. "He didn't have any money."

"Your husband does?"

"Lots."

"I don't believe you. I don't think that's the reason. Why?"

She put the coffee cup down and lit another cigarette. I didn't say anything. Like the government, which collects taxes on the stuff, I could see the benefit. "You're right. There was something strange about Brian. Nothing sinister, as you've been suggesting."

I wasn't aware that I'd been suggesting anything sinister. Maybe that feeling I'd had in the flat was seeping through. "Tell me," I said.

"Brian wasn't completely grown up. I know he'd been widowed and raised a child and held a responsible job and so on, but there was something boyish about him. Attractive, you understand, but . . ."

"I see."

"Not very helpful?"

"I don't know. I'm all at sea when it comes to psychology. Have you any idea why he was like this?"

"Was?"

"Is."

"Not really, unless it's that he lived in the shadow of his father, who was one of the chief engineers for the harbor bridge. I gather that there was some pressure on Brian to become an engineer, but he wasn't interested. His father was a strong personality, apparently. I suppose being a builder of the bridge was a pretty big deal back in the thirties and forties."

"I suppose. I guess fathers have to do something."

"Mmm. Mine made a lot of money. What did yours do, Mr. Hardy?"

"Nothing to be ashamed of," I said. "That's all you can tell me, Mrs. Burton?"

"That's all. What d'you think can have happened to him?"

"I don't know. I'll have to keep digging—try his colleagues, try to get at his bank accounts."

"That's . . . ugly."

The rich tend to think that their money is beautiful but that it's ugly for others to look too closely at it. I decided that there was something a bit hard about Mrs. Burton. Perhaps I let that show. In any case, the rapport between us dissolved. I told her that I'd let her know if I found anything useful. She nodded and put her cigarettes away. We could have been discussing a stolen car. She forced a smile and walked away, her firm, disciplined body steady on her high heels. I didn't think Louise Madden would like her much. I didn't myself; but Brian Madden had, and that was what mattered. My trip to the north shore hadn't worked out so well. I'd turned over some of the physical and personal residues of Brian Mad-

den's life, but I didn't feel that I knew the man
at all.

I'd made some notes while I was in Madden's
flat. I had the name of a travel agency he'd
used when he'd taken a trip to New Caledonia
a few years back, also the name of a Queensland resort he'd stayed at for a week during his
summer vacation. The registration number of
the Laser was in my pocket along with the
names of a solicitor, a doctor, and the high
roller Henry Bush. Threads to pull, and I
pulled them through the rest of the afternoon.
I called at the travel agency and phoned the
resort and got what I expected: nothing. Brian
Madden had done just the one bit of business
with them. From the secretaries to the doctor
and solicitor I got appointments. In return for
a modest financial consideration, I extracted a
promise from a contact in the Department of
Motor Transport to make available all recent
information on the Laser.

When I rang Henry Bush's number, I got his
answering machine: "Hi there! This is Henry
Bush. Sorry I can't talk to you right now, but I
will pronto if you'll leave your name and number after the yodel." A high, trembling Swiss
yodel tickled my eardrums. I was so surprised
I hung up without leaving a message. *That
must happen to a lot of people,* I thought.
Maybe that's why he does it. Anyway, he didn't
sound like the kind of man to commit murder
for ten bucks.

All this took me through to six o'clock and left me in the Crown Hotel in Norton Street, Leichhardt, where you can get a glass of red or white wine for a dollar and the use of a public phone in the bar. I bought my first drink of the day at 6:01 and moved away from the phone. I felt I'd put in a reasonable sort of a day on the Brian Madden case and could now turn my attention to Rhino Jackson. The Crown is right across the straight from one of the gambling places Jackson was reputed to protect. And if he wasn't there, I had a good chance of finding someone who knew where he was. But I was fairly confident of finding him; Jackson was a gambler as well as a protection provider, and gamblers are addicted to the atmosphere of gambling. No other kind of air can sustain their life.

As I drank the glass of one-dollar red, I reflected that everything I knew about Jackson would be known to the police. But in looking for a missing witness, you're not necessarily in competition with the police; it depends how hard they want to find him or her. Sometimes they want to very badly, and then it's the SWOS force and the sledgehammers on the doors at dawn; sometimes they don't, and all that happens is that a few questions get asked and a few forms get filled in. Until I learned more from Parker and Sackville, I had no way of knowing how hard the police were trying. With me it's different; I'm *always* trying hard, usually for the money and in this case for my skin.

I thought about another glass of wine but settled for a light beer and then went across the street to the Bar Napoli, where I had the wine and a lasagna to blot it up. Its being Wednesday night, the place was pretty quiet. I go there often enough to consider myself almost a regular, and I saw a few people I'd seen there before, and that tells you you're a regular. But it's the kind of café you feel comfortable in whether you're a regular or not. The people serving the food and coffee will talk to you if you want or leave you alone—your choice. You can read or look at the nicely framed paintings, drawings, and photographs on the walls. These are by people known to the management and are for sale. I once saw a customer buy a painting.

I ate my food slowly and made the wine last. The television was turned to SBS for the news and a sports roundup, and then Bruno, the proprietor, turned it off and settled down with cigarettes and a short black to talk to his pals. The TV wouldn't go on again unless Bruno said so, and that meant until there was a soccer match. That was fine with me. I read some stories in the *Sydney Review*, a giveaway tabloid that seems to be subsidized by upmarket wineries and boutiques. I got a few laughs and a few yawns for free. Two dawdled-over coffees took me past eight o'clock, which was still way too early to find Rhino Jackson behind a wheel or a poker hand. Before leaving, I had a quick word with Bruno, and we came to an understanding.

I took a walk around the back streets, making the dogs bark but drawing comradely nods from the other nocturnal strollers.

By nine-fifteen I'd run out of streets and was sharp and clearheaded. A plane passed over, low down and with landing lights blinking, as I reached into the car and took out the licensed and totally legal Smith & Wesson .38 automatic. As I put the weapon in the pocket of my leather jacket, I had the thought that 99 percent of the people I'd seen and spoken to since I'd arrived in Leichhardt would have disapproved of my carrying it in their suburb. I disapproved myself, more or less, but there was that dangerous 1 percent who thought and acted differently. It was still too early to find Jackson playing games, but it wasn't too early to ask around, politely.

Four doors down from the Bar Napoli is another coffee shop in which very little coffee seems to get drunk. It's small, crowded with tables, has a big flashy espresso machine, and people work hard at creating a busy atmosphere. The TV is always on; *La Fiamma* and other papers and magazines lie about, and there's always at least one table with coffee cups and full ashtrays sitting on it. They sit there for a long time. Also sitting for a long time is a succession of men who smoke, watch the TV with one eye and the street with the other. In Australian they're called cockatoos; I don't know what they're called in Italian.

I went past the Bar Napoli and gave Bruno the sign. Then I walked into the other place and nodded to the man sitting near the door. There were no other customers, but there was a guy sitting on a stool behind the bar. He was dark and thin, not more than twenty years old, and he was reading an Italian soft-porn magazine with deep concentration. I bought cigarettes I wouldn't smoke and a cappuccino I wouldn't drink from him and put two twenty-dollar notes on the counter. He made change for one of the twenties, and I pushed it and the other note toward him.

"You know me, don't you, mate?" I said.

He shook his head.

I pointed at the door. Bruno stood there, all five feet three and two hundred pounds of him. He nodded, and the man behind the bar scooped up my money. His accent was straight inner-west Sydney. "It's too early," he said.

"I'm looking for someone."

"Who'd that be?"

"Rhino Jackson."

"Haven't seen him for a fuckin' month, the bastard."

"My sentiments exactly. I'll go up and watch for a bit."

He shrugged and went back to his tits and bums. I pushed past a couple of empty tables and went up a set of stairs placed so far back from the light in the room that you couldn't see them from the street. I made out that I could hardly see to climb them; I hung on to the rail and almost stumbled on the first landing. It occurred to me that it wouldn't hurt for the porn freak and anyone else to think I was half drunk or half blind. No one worries about a blind man; no one presses warning buzzers. I pushed open the door at the top of the stairs and walked into the room where they sold plastic chips and scotch rather than cigarettes and cappuccino.

I've been in dozens of such places in my time, and although they all smell the same and share a certain look, each one has something distinctive about it. Some look fixed and established, as if they've been there since federation; others look as if everything could be wheeled out the door and the place turned into a carpet display center inside thirty seconds. This one specialized in European sporting motifs; there were photographs of boxers, cyclists, soccer players, and others on the walls. Most of the sportsmen were Italian, but there were some Yugoslavs among the water polo players and some Austrians among the skiers. In a glass case was a soccer ball signed by a couple of dozen people; an unsigned pair of boots was in another case.

There were about twenty people in the room. A six-handed card game was going strong in one corner, and there were three playing and a couple watching at a baccarat table. Two roulette wheels were yet to attract players and another baccarat dealer was giving himself a hand of patience while he awaited customers.

Four men were rolling dice under the eye of a large character who slightly resembled one of the photos on the wall—the one of Primo Carnera. His dark, hooded eyes followed me as I moved around the room. I stopped at the bar and bought some chips and a scotch and soda. This seemed to comfort Primo, who went back to concentrating on the rolling dice. There was a little talk, not much, some drinking and cigar smoking going on, not much. The place was just warming up, like a car with the motor running but no gears engaged.

I took my chips to a roulette wheel and lost them in fairly rapid order.

"Bad luck," said the croupier, a small, sleek-haired character starting to look old before he was thirty.

"Have you seen Rhino Jackson lately?"

He inspected the end of his spatula and picked off a piece of fluff. "I didn't think you were a serious player. Cop?"

"No. Who would I talk to about who comes in here and who doesn't?"

The croupier grinned. "Not me, that's for sure. Why don't you try him?" He jerked his head at Primo.

I wandered away from the table with my drink and thought about that. I had the distinct feeling that talking wasn't Primo's long suit and that if I insisted, he'd roll me down the stairs just to keep his wrist in practice. I was on the point of buying more chips when a party of a dozen or so, including four or five women, came in. Immediately the place seemed to pick up a glow. The noise level went up, people starting buying drinks and jostling good-naturedly for position at the tables.

I had to queue for my chips. The door opened, and Lou Campisi walked in. Lou had been a jockey until he grew too big; then he played league for a while, but he proved to be too small. His middle-sized physique had done the dirty on him twice. It might have embittered some men, but Lou took it in his stride. He went energetically into SP bookmaking, race fixing, supplying illegal drugs to football players, and scalping finals tickets. Anywhere there was a quick, soiled dollar to be made out of racing and football, Lou was on the spot. He was also an associate of Jackson's. They probably discussed electric saddles and quick counts, ring-ins, and tank jobs together. I bought my chips, fifty dollars' worth this time instead of the previous ten, and moved away quickly so that Campisi wouldn't see me.

Watching an addicted gambler play is a bit like watching an alcoholic drink. You know he enjoys it up to a point; but that point quickly passes, and simple need takes over. Campisi was drinking steadily and losing. He made several trips to the chip desk, and his original plunging style gave way to a more cautious approach. All this meant was that he lost more slowly. Toward the end he started to get a bit desperate; he had a winning run at baccarat; but it soon petered out, and I moved in on him when I calculated that the two chips in his hand were his last.

"Hello, Lou," I said. "How's tricks?"

He turned his bleary loser's eyes on me. "Lousy. Who're you?"

"You remember me, Lou. Cliff Hardy. I helped to unfix one of your fixes a few years ago." Three years before, to be precise, when I'd been employed by a horse trainer to find out who was bribing his riders.

"Push off, prick," Campisi said.

I showed him my stack of chips. "Lose the ones you've got there, and then come over and see me. These could be yours."

"I'm winning, cunt."

"You'll never win, Lou. You just play. Go ahead, play."

He placed the chips on the red and lost. I'd moved back to watch him. He went through his pockets, first for chips, then for money. He came up empty. A woman at the roulette wheel gave a shriek as her ball dropped in. Campisi wet his lips and looked around for me. He saw me, hesitated, lit a cigarette, and came across.

"You got some kind of a proposition, Hardy?"

I moved across to the wall farthest from Primo, and Campisi followed me. "Yes, there's something you could help me with, if you've a mind to."

Another squeal from the roulette table where a knot of people had gathered. Campisi glanced across. "Wheel's running hot."

"You could get in on it." I clinked the chips together.

"What do you want?"

"Information. Solid, factual information. The kind that checks out or I come back and point out to you that you made a big mistake."

"Sure. Sure. You're tough. What d'you want to know?"

"Where to find Rhino Jackson. Tonight."

Campisi wet his lips. "I don't know. I—"

Clink. Clink. "Yes, you do."

He was tempted but very afraid. The noise in the room had mounted, along with the level of smoke and the fumes of whiskey; the women's perfume was giving the air an extra tang. To addicts such as Lou Campisi it was like the kiss of life. He wanted to go on breathing it, suck it in deeper, but . . .

He shook his head. "I don't know where he is."

The reluctance in his voice told me that he did know and something else: He almost wanted me to force him to tell. I gripped the .38 in my pocket and lifted it up a few inches so that Campisi could see it. "Feel like knocking this place over with me, Lou? We could do it."

He turned pale, and the hand holding the

cigarette for nonchalance shook violently. "Are you crazy? Get away from me!"

I held his arm and kept him from backing off. "Listen, Rhino's trying to put me out of business. I go up in front of a court next week and I'm history. But it's just a misunderstanding. We can sort it out."

He wavered. "I dunno . . ."

"If this thing goes through and they lift my license, I'm done for. I can't make a living. I'd just as soon take what they've got in here and blow. Leave Sydney. Go north with a big piece of cash."

"You're crazy. This place is protected. Look at that big cunt over there. One man couldn't handle him."

"Two," I said.

"No."

I sniffed and let a wild look come into my eyes. "I'm going to do it, and you're in."

"No, no! Shit, Hardy. Take your hand outa your pocket. All right, all right. I'll tell you where Jackson is. Just back down, will you?"

I let him see both hands and began tossing the chips from one to the other. "Yes, Lou?"

"You won't let on it was me told you?"

"Lou, would I?"

"An' you'll give me the chips?"

"You're doing an awful lot of asking, Lou, and not giving anything."

"He's on a houseboat."

"That's nice. Where?"

"I don't know. It moves around."

"Come on, Lou. You're playing games. The wheel's going to go cold on you."

"Look, all I know is, he's in partnership with Reg Bailey, who's an ex-cop, like him. They've got this houseboat with all the gambling gear on it—high-class stuff. It moves around. Goes from one, what d'you call it?"

"Mooring?"

"Right. From one mooring to another. What the fuck do I know? From Palm Beach to . . . anywhere on the fuckin' harbor. I've never been on it. It's a top-class thing—trainers, owners, politicians, doctors—big money."

Lou's association of certain professions with big money would have been of interest to sociologists; for me it gave his statement the ring of truth. But not the ring of helpfulness. I let the chips stay in one hand and closed my fist over them.

"Hardy," Lou said, "that's all I know."

"Boats have names, Lou. Even houseboats. Give me the name, and we're in business."

"Fuck you."

"They wouldn't register that."

"The *Paravotti*."

"What?"

"*Paravotti*, *Pavarotti*, like that. Bailey's some kind of music nut, I heard. The boat's named after an opera or somethin'. Hardy . . ."

I poured the chips into Campisi's sweaty palm. "Thanks, Lou," I said. "Big help."

"Fuck you."

7

I WENT BACK TO THE CROWN, GOT HOLD OF ANOTHER GLASS OF DOLLAR RED, AND THE yellow pages. Ten years ago I'd have been able to telephone all the marinas on the harbor, but not now. At a rough count there were about a hundred of them. Some weren't possibilities, of course—glorified boatsheds where you couldn't tie up anything much bigger than a dinghy. But there were still too many imposing-sounding ones—Middle Harbour Moorings, Peninsula Marina, Clearwater Luxury Marina—that could, presumably, accommodate a houseboat, to make a ring-around possible.

Paul Guthrie was a client from a few years back. He'd been an Olympic sculler and later a successful businessman. A satisfied client, as it had turned out, he was quite big in boating circles and might know where you'd tie up a houseboat if you happened to have one. The trouble was I didn't know whether he was still alive. Too often these days when I ring old clients, I get recent widows. But I dredged his address up from my memory and found him still listed in the telephone book. Not proof of existence—some widows never change the listing—but encouraging.

I sat by the same phone as before, fed in the money, and punched the buttons. Guthrie's brisk, no-nonsense voice sounded impatient but was just an indicator of his energy.

"Paul Guthrie."

"Cliff Hardy, Mr. Guthrie. You might remember—"

"Of course I remember, Cliff. Of course I do. How the hell are you? You said you'd drop in on us, but you never did."

He was right; I always say it, and I never do. "I'm sorry. I've been busy, I guess. How are the boys?" I referred to his two adopted sons, both in trouble at one time.

"Just fine. Me 'n' Pat're grandparents. But you don't want to hear about that. I hope you want some help. God knows I'd like to do something for you after what you did for us."

"I'm glad you feel that way. It's not a big thing. I'm looking for a houseboat called the *Pavarotti*. I don't suppose you know it?"

"No." There was a lot of regret in the word. "I don't get out on the water much these days. Getting a bit stiff for it."

"Sorry to hear it. I wonder if you could tell me the marinas that could take such a thing? I gather it's pretty big."

"Sure, I've got a pretty good idea, and Ray's here, he'd have an even better one. Can I call you back, Cliff?"

"No. I'm in a pub. I could call you again in, what, fifteen minutes."

"Make it ten. In a pub, eh? Still no home-life? What happened to that woman you met? Hannah?"

"Helen," I said. "It's a long story. Say hello to Ray for me. I'll ring back in ten minutes."

I still had an inch of wine left. As I drank it, I tried to think about the good things, about helping Guthrie out of his trouble, trying to keep thoughts of Helen at a distance. To deal with *those* thoughts, I'd have needed a good deal more help than an inch of cask red. When Guthrie came back on the line, he sounded pleased.

"Ray knows the boat. He's seen it quite a few times. Says it's a flashy number with a good deal of rot in the hull."

"Does he know where it is now?"

"No, but he can find out for you first thing in the morning."

I gave him the home and office numbers and got a number for Ray in return. We exchanged a few more pleasantries and I promised again to visit him and Pat in Cammeray. Maybe this time I would.

All things considered, it looked as if I were

through for the night. But you can't be too sure. I hung around outside the gambling joint until Lou Campisi staggered out. He had to root around in his pockets for cab fare, and since he was drunk, this made a pantomime which would have been amusing if you didn't know that the man had been a good jockey and a good fly half. I tailed the taxi, partly to check whether Lou might have had pangs of conscience or pocket that might take him to see Jackson, drunk and all as he was. Also, it never hurts to stay in practice.

But the petrol was wasted. The taxi dropped Lou in Newtown; there was an argument about the fare, and then Lou reeled through the gate and up the steps of a boardinghouse. After a struggle he got a key into the lock and went inside. Lou was tucked up safe for the night, Jackson was sporting himself in a floating casino, and my head was hurting again. I was glad Ray didn't have the location of the *Pavarotti* to hand; I didn't feel up to a row or a swim.

I slept for six hours. That meant I was up and making coffee as it started to get light. The house was cold, and I turned on heaters and waited for the morning paper to hit the front door. I collected it and tore the front page getting the wrapper off. The tear went right through a report on the bad balance of payments figures and saved me from having to read it. I picked my way through the rest of the paper without much interest until I spotted a small item on page four. It was headed BODY FOUND IN HARBOR. Apparently the body of a man had been fished out of the water at Dawes Point. As yet unidentified, the body was of a middle-aged man of average build with no distinguishing marks. That gave me something to think about while I ate toast, shaved, drank more coffee, and waited for Ray Guthrie's call.

"Mr. Hardy?" It was the voice I remembered: private school overlaid by the accents picked up in a working life as a boat charterer and repairer.

"Call me Cliff, Ray. How are you?"

"Just fine. I located that houseboat for you, the *Pavarotti*. Good name, lousy boat."

"Where is it?"

"Darling Point."

I had the yellow pages open again and ran my finger down the listings. "I can't see a marina there."

"It's not at a marina, more of a private jetty. One of the few left around there."

"It must be a big jetty."

"Big house, big garden, big jetty. Can you tell me why you're interested, Cliff? I hope you're not planning to buy it."

I laughed. "You wouldn't advise it?"

"No way. It looks good from a distance, probably looks its best at night, but it's got lots of problems."

"I'm told it moves around the harbor a bit."

"One of these days it'll move down." Ray

was smart enough to see that I wasn't going to answer his question and secure enough not to be offended. He'd married his childhood sweetheart, had a son and a daughter and a good business; why shouldn't he be secure? Still, he'd had a wild phase once, and wild men never completely calm down. "Do you need any help? Like to approach from the water side, perhaps? I'd be happy to . . ."

I thanked him but refused. He told me that the houseboat had been at Darling Point for two days and that it generally stayed for a week at wherever it tied up. More thanks from me and a reluctant "See you" from him. I had to be careful. How did it go again? "A licensed private enquiry agent shall not employ in any way whatsoever in connection with his business as a subagent any person who is not a licensed subagent." Section 19(1) or thereabouts.

The day had started cold and wasn't going to warm up much. The sky was clear, with some clouds over in the west; the wind seemed to be blowing gently from all quarters; anything could happen. I wore a sweater under my jacket, and when I tried to stuff a scarf into a pocket, I found the gun still there. I put the gun away in the glove box of the car, but no matter how hard you try you always end up breaking the rules: I wasn't keeping my notes on the Madden case up-to-date. I should have made an entry before I set off: "to morgue to view body found in harbor."

Proximity to the Arundel Street morgue is not one of the reasons I live in Glebe. I've visited the liver-colored brick building more often than I care to remember, and it doesn't improve on acquaintance: too clean, too smooth, too final. I filled in a form and showed my threatened license to an attendant, who noted my name down carefully on a list that carried three other names.

"What's that for?" I said.

The attendant, a young Asian man in a white coat who had several medical textbooks on his desk, looked up at me over the tops of his half-moon glasses. "For the police. They want the name of everyone who views the body."

"Good," I said.

The would-be doctor passed me on to another attendant, an older, tired-looking individual, who showed me through several sets of heavy Perspex doors down artificially lit corridors to the chamber where the bodies are stored. It's like you see in the movies, except that the refrigerated compartments pull out widthwise rather than lengthwise, like a crisper drawer. The attendant, who wore thick rubber gloves, undid two clasps and slid the drawer out a few inches.

"Hands clear," he said.

I clasped my hands behind me like the duke of Edinburgh and leaned forward to look. The deceased was naked, bloated, and blue. The body carried a lot of wounds and what I took to be bruises—dark, pulpy discolorations on the shoulders and thighs and around the wrists and ankles.

"Glass bottom," the attendant said, "if you want to look at the back."

"Like on the Barrier Reef," I said.

He didn't smile, and I didn't need to look at the back of the corpse; the man had been of shorter, blockier build than Brian Madden and had lacked his thick pepper-and-salt hair. Bald, anonymous, and dead. There's not much to say about a corpse that's been in the water awhile. It's as if the sea has wiped away status, career, personality, history, the lot. I shook my head, and the drawer slid back with scarcely a sound. The label on the front read "DROWNED MALE."

The attendant moved a plastic bucket aside with his foot. He'd had it all ready to bring into use. He looked almost apologetic. "You've done this before," he said.

"Yes."

"So had the last copper who was here. Didn't matter. I still had to use the bucket."

We held the door open, and we went out into the corridor, where the air was warmer but still smelled of death. "The police are interested in this one, are they?" I said.

He shrugged. Maybe he only liked to talk about buckets.

Back at the desk I surprised the aspiring medico running a pink marker pen through a paragraph in a physiology textbook. He looked guilty. "Important passage," he said.

"Good luck to you. Can you give me the name of the policeman who asked you to keep that list?"

He tapped his teeth with the pen. "Sergeant Meredith."

"Did he leave you his number?"

"I think so." He searched among the books, pens, papers, and used tissues on his desk, examined several slips of paper with writing on them, but shook his head each time. "I can't find it, but it doesn't matter. He's due in now with someone to look at the body. You can talk to him in person."

"Meredith's personally bringing someone in to look at the body?"

"Yes, probably a relative."

"I showed you my private enquiry agent license before."

"You did."

"I'm working on a missing persons case."

"I guessed that. Not your subject in the drawer, eh?"

"No. What makes you think the sergeant's got hold of a relative?"

"I think he said so on the phone. He's a pleasant chap. We've talked a bit. I've a knack for getting people to talk. When I'm a doctor . . ."

"Which I'm sure you will be."

"Thank you. It could be useful."

"Certainly. Do you know why the police are so interested in this body, doctor?"

He let go one of the few smiles the place would see all day. "I heard the sergeant say something about another bridge case. I didn't know what that meant. The harbor bridge, I assume. But those injuries aren't consistent with a fall. . . ."

I didn't hear the rest of what he said. I was out through the door and down the steps, looking along the street for a place to hide. I stood in a shop doorway near the Ross Street corner and watched a young, smartly dressed man climb out of a red Holden Commodore, open the back door, and escort a small middle-aged woman to the steps of the morgue. Another car drew up, parked illegally, and a big man in a rumpled suit got out and joined the pair on the steps. They went in, and I waited. When they came out, the woman was distressed, leaning on the young man's arm and holding a handkerchief to her face. The other man, whom I'd tagged as Meredith by now, talked briefly with them, patted the woman's shoulder, and went off to his car. I scooted down the street for mine and was sitting in it, ready to go left or right, when the Commodore, moving slowly as if it were already part of a funeral procession, turned out of Arundel Street.

The Commodore turned left into Parramatta Road, and I had to skip through a second of red light to stay behind. A bad start. Do that to someone who suspects he's being followed, and it's like turning on a siren. But the Commodore driver didn't react. He drove steadily in the center lane up past the railway and through Surry Hills until he picked up the freeway to the eastern suburbs. A good, considerate driver—the easiest kind to follow. I stayed modestly back, moving up occasionally to catch a light, but not getting any closer than I needed to. I made a mental note of the registration number and tried to guess where we would end up. I plumped for Bondi Junction and was almost right, but on the low side, sociologically. The Commodore slid down the leafy driveway beside a block of flats in Birriga Road, Bellevue Hill.

I stopped farther up the curving, rising road and walked back to the flats. It was an old block of about ten apartments that had once commanded a majestic harbor view at the back. Even from the road you could see that the modern multilevel building had whittled this away. Still, a bijou address, especially with the off-street parking. The Commodore was parked in the space along the side of the wide driveway marked "6." I stood around contemplating my next move when a white Jaguar cruised noiselessly up and stopped fair and square across the entrance to the drive.

It was my day for crossing roads and taking cover. I stood behind a VW van parked on the other side of the road and saw a white-haired man get out of the Jaguar and help the woman

I'd seen at the morgue into the back of the car. The young man was there, too, patting people and murmuring things, but he stayed behind as the Jag drove off. He held a respectful attitude until it was out of sight, and then he seemed to loosen up. His step on the way back down the drive was almost jaunty. The wind was blowing leaves along the footpath, and a gust pushed a heap of them up against my feet. *Some detective,* I thought. *Stands around being late autumnal while things are happening.* Breaking in on bereavement is one thing, but if the man with the red Commodore had been bereaved, he'd got over it awfully fast.

Flat 6 was on the second level at the back. The entrance was through a handsome door in a tiled, balustraded porch. It was one of those doors that were opened electrically from inside the flats, but it wasn't locked. I looked down and saw that the door had snagged on a piece of uplifted carpet, just enough to prevent the lock from engaging. Conclusion: The young man didn't live here and didn't know that you had to give the door a shove to get the security you were paying for. I went into a quiet, cool lobby with cream walls and dark timber and up a flight of stairs. I tried to give my knock on the door of number 6 the authority that brooks no denial.

The man who answered the door was middle-sized and fair in coloring except for his slightly flushed face. He'd taken off his suit jacket and loosened his tie. He held an opened bottle of champagne in one hand. "What do you want?" he said.

I flashed the license folder quicker than a camera shutter. "My name's Hardy. Sergeant Meredith asked me to have a quick word with you."

The familiar name did the trick. He eased back, and I was partway through the door before an objection occurred to him. "He didn't say anything to my mother or me back at the morgue."

I fished out my notebook and leafed through, still inching my way in. "Well, he knew your mother'd be distressed. Now you are Mr. . . . ?"

"Clive Glover." He held up the bottle. "I suppose this looks bad?"

"I don't know, sir. Not necessarily. Could we go inside? Thank you. Now your mother made a formal identification of?"

We moved down the passage into a large sitting room with a kitchen off it to one side and another passage that probably led to bedrooms. "My father, Mr. Colin Glover. Yes."

He sat down in an easy chair in front of an elaborate marble-edged fireplace. A half-filled tulip-shaped champagne glass was sitting on the tiles in front of the grate. I looked around the room, which showed signs of affluence, taste, and an orientation toward the past. The furniture was expensive but old; the decorations owed nothing to modern ideas of design.

One item was of more interest to me than

others—of great interest. I'd missed it at first because the bright late-morning light, coming in from a window that gave the depleted view of the harbor, struck the glass and obliterated the image. I moved a little and could see it. Hanging over the fireplace was a large photograph in a heavy black frame. The picture was of the last stage of construction of the Sydney Harbour Bridge.

8

"WELL, I DON'T CARE. I HATED THE OLD BASTARD."

"Mr. Glover?"

He leaned forward, filled a glass, lifted it, and drained the contents. Then he poured another and sipped. "My father. I'm glad they found him, and I'm glad they found him dead. Being missing was no good to me."

I sat down on a two-seater couch without being invited. I probably wouldn't have refused a glass of champagne, but Glover seemed intent on drinking the whole bottle himself. He was a nervy type, I decided—inclined to be loudmouthed and assertive but really pretty unsure of himself. I noticed that his fingers were heavily nicotine-stained a millisecond before he rummaged in the pocket of the jacket he'd dumped on the back of his chair and pulled out a packet of Senior Service. He lit up and sucked the smoke deep. There was no ashtray around. It wasn't the sort of room where you expected to find one.

"I don't think I understand," I said.

"I'm not going to make a secret of it. My father was ruining the business. He wouldn't listen to me when I said I could save it because he said only engineers understand engineering."

"And you are?"

"An accountant. He was wrong. I knew how to save the business. Now I can do it."

I really wasn't interested. All I wanted to do was ask about the photograph, but I'd got myself into an odd situation. Usually, quickly assumed disguises are seen through quickly and you're lucky if you get your couple of questions across. Glover seemed to want to believe I was a cop and to talk, but he'd wake up sooner or later. "The engineering firm, I see. Would that account for the photograph? An engineering marvel, the bridge."

He glanced up at the photograph, and a look of contempt came over his face. "So everyone seems to think. I've heard nothing but 'Grandpa built the bridge' since I was knee-high. I never go over the bloody thing myself unless I have to. I hope it falls down. Probably will one day."

"Your grandfather built the bridge?" I couldn't keep the surprise and inquisitiveness out of my voice.

"He was one of the engineers, yes. I . . ." He drew on his cigarette and used the action to give himself time to think. Also, probably, to take a good look at me: leather jacket, no tie, broken nose, and hair that needed cutting. "Could I see your ID again?"

"Just a few more questions, sir, and I'll be on my way. Your father went missing when?"

"A couple of weeks ago. I want to see the ID."

I reached into my pocket. "What's the name of the firm?"

"You're not a policeman."

"I never said I was. You assumed it."

"You said Sergeant Meredith—"

"I lied. I don't want to make trouble for you, Mr. Glover. You can take over the firm and build Meccano sets for all I care. I just want some information."

"I've nothing to say."

"How would your mother react if I got her across here and she found you with the champers open?"

"How could you do that?"

I got up, standing as tall as I could, and went across the room to the telephone. "I got the number of the Jag. Two calls, and I've got the phone number of the silver-haired gent it's registered to. One more call, and I'm on to your mum."

"Who are you?"

"I told you at the door. You let me in, re-member? Come on, Mr. Glover. Be smart. A couple of questions and I'm gone and you can open another bottle and get a couple of girls in. What's the name of the firm?"

"That's one question. Glover and Barclay."

"Who's Barclay?"

"Two. He was a partner. Son of the original Barclay, like my father was son of the original Glover."

"Why do you say 'was'?"

"That's three questions."

I picked up the phone.

"Okay, okay. He's dead. He was killed a few years ago by a hit-and-run driver."

"Where?"

"On an approach to the bridge. It was in the papers. Bridge builder's son killed on father's creation, that sort of crap."

I dropped the phone. The noise made him jump. Nervy, just as I thought. I put my notebook away and walked out of the room and down the passage. I heard the bottle clink against the rim of the glass just before the door closed behind me. I'd spoiled his day, but I can't say I was sorry. I flattened the carpet and let the door lock; then I pressed the buzzer for flat 6. Nothing happened, and I pressed it again. When Glover's shaky voice came over the intercom, I said nothing and walked away. The more distracted Mr. Glover was, the less likely he was to remember a name and a face. Impersonating a police officer was a charge I didn't want to have to think about.

* * *

I drove down to Bondi to eat fish and chips on the grass and look out over the water. That was the plan, but the cold wind drove me to eat the food in the car and to look at the water through the windshield. Modern life—we see more of the world on film than with our eyes, and more and more of our experience is coming at second hand, through experts, commentators, and communicators. I think it must have been a communicator on the radio who told me that. As I munched the food, I looked out at the deep blue water, breaking up into whitecaps three hundred feet out and rolling into the bleak, empty beach. The water looked clean, but we're told it isn't. It wasn't the kind of day to go down and find out.

But the water led me to thoughts of the harbor and the bridge and on from there to consideration of Detective Sergeant Meredith. I didn't recall any clause in the act that compelled the licensed private enquiry agent to cooperate with the police, but there often comes a point when that's the right course of action. The problem is to judge when the moment is right. Go too early and the cops can shut you out completely; go too late and they can do you for obstruction or worse. I judged, as I usually do, that it was too early.

I dumped the lunch leavings in a rubbish bin and drove back to Darlinghurst. Another stroll down William Street and through Hyde Park took me to the city library in Pitt Street. The library has one of those idiot-proof computer systems where you read the instructions off the screen, touch a marker beside the entry you want, and find your way home. I ended up with *The Sydney Harbour Bridge* by Peter Spearritt and *Building the Sydney Harbour Bridge: The Photography of Henry Mallard* as the most useful-looking items. The fact that both were on the shelves meant my luck was running strongly this day. The photographs were well worth an hour or so: clear and sharp images, unsentimental, a tremendous record of a tremendous feat. The last photograph in the book showed the photographer himself sitting on a heap of metal high above the water. He wore a suit and hat, and you could just see the tip of his waxed mustache. Probably the engineers, Bradfield, Barclay, Glover, Madden, and others looked much the same.

Spearritt's book was a detailed, readable study of the bridge, from the germ of the idea to build one through all the politicking and chicanery that necessarily followed. He had a ton of information on the actual construction from the technical and human points of view and chapters on the impact the bridge made on the life of the city. I wished I had time to read it all. Spearritt was no whitewash merchant. He discussed the plight of people who had lost their homes as a result of the construction, and he had a chapter on those who had actually been killed on the job. Sixteen of them, apparently, mostly riveters, but the casualty list included painters, quarrymen, and others. One sentence on page 68 took my eye: "Safety regulations scarcely existed, and it is amazing that there were not many more deaths."

I copied a few pages, including the photograph of the almost closed arch, which lost a lot in the reproduction but still constituted part of my evidence. I sat back in my chair in front of the empty screen. Computers are wonderful, but they can't actually help you to think. If I entered into a database what I had—two dead engineers and one missing plus a policeman mentioning "bridge cases" and supposing there was a key marked "Conclusions" —what would I get? My own conclusion was "What else have you got?"

I scrolled back through the catalog entries in case I'd missed something and came across a pamphlet entitled *Your Bridge, Our History.* One of the librarians discovered it in a filing case, after a search that threatened to turn into a major stocktaking. The pamphlet was just a few pages stapled together. It was published a few years back by something called the Veterans of the Bridge Society. It contained a couple of reminiscences from men who had worked on the bridge, a couple of Mallard's photographs, a list of the men killed and seriously injured in the course of the work, and a selection of opinions from ordinary people. Some praised the bridge as an engineering marvel; others condemned it for ruining the Rocks area and Circular Quay. The secretary of the Veterans of the Bridge Society was Stan Livermore, and the pamphlet carried his address: 43A Pump Street, The Rocks.

All this had taken me a couple of hours, but I hadn't spent much of Louise Madden's money. I hadn't even got a receipt for the photocopies. So a cab to the Rocks seemed not unreasonable.

We pulled up near enough to the Argyle Centre for me to feel that with the best will in the world, restorers and preservers have an uphill battle. The old buildings were too clean, too sanitized to be convincing, even though every stone in them was original and genuine. Still, since leaving it alone isn't an option, cleaning it up is better than tearing it down. Around a couple of corners in Pump Street things changed for the better or the worse, depending on your point of view. The narrow houses seemed to be holding one another up, and for decades corroded guttering and downpipes had leaked rusty water across stones and cement, leaving a brown stain that would never wear away. Though none of the buildings was more than two stories high, they blocked out the late-afternoon sunshine so that the street was cold and gloomy. No trees, no front gardens sprouting wattle. This was more like the old Rocks: convict-built, working class–inhabited, drink-loving, and police-hating. A large red brick warehouse or bond store dominated the end of the street.

A man in a heavy overcoat turned out of a

lane ahead of me and hurried along the narrow footpath. The street was lined with terrace houses, and he disappeared into one of them, maybe number 43A, maybe the house next door, I couldn't be sure. Number 43A was a skinny sandstone terrace, one of five built so that you stepped directly from the front door onto the footpath. The balcony above had been boxed in with asbestos-cement and dimpled glass louvers. The door was scarred at the bottom by generations of collisions with solid boots, and its locks had been changed so many times that the area around the present one was composed of as much old, cracked putty and paint as wood. I knocked and then rubbed my hands together. It was cold in Pump Street, really cold. I jammed my hands into my pockets and waited. A few cars cruised by, and a man carrying a half carton of beer weaved across the street and went into the house at the end of the terrace. To gain admittance, he kicked at the bottom of the door. I was getting nowhere and considered trying a kick. I knocked again and heard a shuffling inside.

"Yes?"

I had to look a long way down to see the face of the woman who had opened the door a few inches. Even then it was hard. She was a tiny, bent figure with white hair, and her back was so bowed the unbuttoned cardigan she wore hung almost to the floor. She turned her head sideways to look up at me—ancient eyes in a face so lined and wrinkled that it looked like an ill-fitting rubber mask. Her head sat stiffly at an odd angle to her shoulders, and she had to swivel the upper part of her body to change her line of vision.

"I'm looking for Stan Livermore," I said. "Does he live here?"

She poked a yellow, arthritic claw out from the greasy turned-back sleeve of the cardigan. "Five dollars."

"What?"

"I ask everyone who knocks at my bloody door for five dollars. You'd be surprised how many pay up."

I paid up in coins. She waited patiently while I collected the amount. She stuffed the money in a pocket of the cardigan and shuffled back. "Just a minute," I said. "I asked you about Mr Livermore."

"Old Stan?"

"That's right."

"Silly old bugger."

The idea of this crone's emphasizing the fact of someone else's age struck me as funny, and I smiled.

"What're you laughing at?"

Even with her head turned like that, dry, moth-eaten hair hanging in her face and the skin around them warty and puckered like a toad's, the eyes were still serving her. "Nothing," I said. "Look, madam, it's terribly cold out here. Could I come in?"

"You might rape me."

"I won't, I assure you." I showed her my license, as if a piece of paper were some kind of guarantee against rape.

"Hardy," she said, reading the license from a distance of a couple of feet. "Knew a woman named Hardy once. Silly bitch."

"Mrs.?"

"Tracey, Betty Tracey. Have you got five dollars?"

"I already gave you five dollars. They're in your pocket."

I was suddenly aware of sounds around and above me. A door had opened in the next house, and a couple of the louver windows had been operated. I guessed what was going on: Old Betty was putting on her show for an always appreciative audience. It was called "Make the stranger look like an idiot," and it ran for as many acts as he was dopey enough to allow. I didn't feel like playing. I took out a twenty-dollar note and waved it in front of Betty's forty-five-degree face. Suddenly she was the bit player and I was the lead. I snapped the note. "If you want this, invite me in."

She stepped back and let the door open wide enough to let me as well as my money pass through it. But that was as much as she was willing to concede. She let the door sit ajar and moved only a few feet down the hallway. There was almost no light; I had an impression of narrow, steep stairs at the end of the passage and one room off to the right.

"Are you going to give me the money or rape

me? Did you see that Lady Whatshername got raped? She was older than me."

She was referring to a wealthy titled north shore woman whose life had ended the way no one's should: raped, robbed, bashed to death. The recollection made me disinclined to any kind of coercion. Risking the chance that she'd suddenly stand up straight and waltz away up the stairs, I handed her the twenty. "I want to talk to Stan Livermore. I was given this as his address. Does he live here?"

"Old Stan?"

Oh, Christ, not again, I thought. "Yes, old Stan. Is he here?"

"No."

'Does he live here?"

She folded the note three times and put it in the pocket along with the coins. "Yes."

"Where is he now?"

She sucked in a deep breath and sniffed. Slowly she swiveled her head around in a ninety-degree turn so that instead of looking up with her head cocked toward her right shoulder, it was cocked toward her left. The maneuver seemed to take a full minute. When she was ready, she sniffed again and wiped her nose on her sleeve. "What's the time?"

Here we go, I thought. I looked at my watch. "Nearly half past four."

"You've got about three-quarters of an hour to catch him then."

"What d'you mean?"

"I know where he'll be till quarter past five;

after that it's anybody's guess. Might come back here tonight, might not."

"Right. Understood. Where will he be until five-fifteen?"

She paused, and I waited for more sniffs, more citations of rape cases, or more requests for money. Maybe she considered all three, but she settled for a sniff. "He'll be in the Botanic Gardens, watching the bloody sun go down behind the bloody bridge. Does it every day it isn't pissing down rain. Silly old bugger."

"So he's still the secretary of this Veterans of the Bridge thing?"

"Course he is. All he thinks about. Him and a coupla others just as mad."

"Where in the gardens?"

She shrugged, which in her case was more of a horizontal movement than a vertical one. "Anywhere he can get a good view. Could be Mrs. Macquarie's Chair, could be closer to the opera house. Anywhere. Took me to see it once. Silly old bugger. Sun goin' down behind the bloody bridge. So what?"

I was moving toward the door, calculating time and distance. "How will I recognize him?"

"Old Stan? Easy, only one of his kind in captivity. White beard down to here." She bunched her cardigan together at the waist. The coins fell out on the floor. Well, she didn't have far to go to pick them up. I hit the foot-path running.

* * *

Getting a cab in the Rocks at half past four in the afternoon is no easy matter, especially when a cold wind has started to blow. That's how it was as I ran along Pump Street toward the nearest corner. No luck; a bus and some private cars threw muddy water from the recently passed street sweeper over my feet. I ran in the direction of the nearest set of lights and moved from one corner of the intersection to the other, trying to second-guess the traffic stream. It took ten minutes, but I finally grabbed a Legion cab which was stopped at the lights. I overcame the driver's reluctance with another twenty-dollar note; Louise Madden was spending some serious money now.

As well as muggers and drunk vomiters, taxi drivers dislike passengers who don't know where they're going and passengers who do know and tell them street by street how to get there. I wanted the Botanic Gardens, and the only instruction I could give was "The nearest gate."

He dropped me opposite the old State Library building, and I battled the wind past the fountain, which wasn't spurting, and through the gate. A newish sign inside told me that this was the Morshead Fountain gate and that the gardens this month were closed to the public at 5:00 P.M. I took the first path that seemed to promise a view of the bridge, almost fell on the first long set of steps, and dashed past another fountain and several statues of Greek gods doing godlike things.

The sky was clear and rapidly turning pink and orange in the west as the sun sank—a good bridge-viewing sky. I had no idea of where the best vantage points would be, and the bridge itself kept disappearing behind trees as I hurried along the paths. A few people straggling up toward the south gate looked at me oddly as I bustled along. The light was fading fast, and the wind's cutting edge seemed to get keener by the minute. I kept heading toward the higher ground, and some instinct or memory told me that keeping the duck pond and kiosk on my right was the proper thing to do.

An avenue of thick, high-reaching palms blocked my view of everything and brought visibility down to murky. Ever since an eye accident a few years ago I've had trouble adapting quickly to changes in light level, and the sudden brightness of direct sunrays that hit the gardens as I emerged from the avenue almost blinded me. I stopped, shaded my eyes, and scanned the lawns and flower beds. For a moment I thought that a rotunda up ahead might provide a good view, but then I realized that a stand of trees was in the way. I moved to the left and got a clear view through a gap in the trees. A path a little farther along led toward a rise in the land and a garden bench. From the bench there would be a clear view through the trees west to the bridge. There was no one on the bench, but a shape lay on the ground beside it. I hurdled a plot of native something or others and ran across the grass to the bench.

He was lying on his back, very still, a thin, frail figure with a big overcoat spread out around him. The long white beard hung down below the V neck of a torn and darned red sweater. The beard was red, too, in the places where blood from the gash on his forehead had splashed onto it. His old pale blue eyes were open, and so was his mouth; a bottom denture had fallen out, and the lower part of his face had a puckered, eroded look. I bent down and felt his thin wrist and put my watch face near his nose and mouth, but there was no pulse and no breath. People say things like "The body was still warm"; that doesn't make much sense on a cold night. His hands and face were as cold as mine. I looked up and saw the bridge etched clearly against the sunset. It was the first time I'd ever seen it, but Stan Livermore would never see it again.

I had no doubt that the dead man was Livermore. In the fading light I could see a lot of blood on the grass, but no signs of a struggle or a weapon. There was more blood and a few hairs on the edge of the bench; a cloth cap lay on the grass a few feet from the body. A pair of spectacles was half covered by the spread skirt of the overcoat. A fall, then? An old, nearsighted man lost his footing, fell, and struck his head? Happens every day. I looked up as a uniformed man came running along the path in the direction opposite from the way I'd come. He was heavy, red-faced, and breathless when he reached the spot.

"Oh, Gawd," he said, "it's old Stan."

I straightened up. "You know him?"

"Yeah." He pulled down the waistband of his uniform jacket, which had ridden up as he ran. The jacket had flashes bearing the word *Ranger* sewn onto the sleeves and the breast pocket. "I know him. Well, we just call him old Stan. Don't know his full name. Comes in every night to watch the sun going down behind the bridge. Done it for years. Poor old bugger must've taken a tumble."

He peered at the bench and saw the blood. Then he unhooked a walkie-talkie from his belt and put in a call for an ambulance.

"He's dead," I said.

"Just following procedure, sir. Could I have your name, please?"

It was the walkie-talkie that did for me. If he'd had to go off somewhere to sound the alert, I might have faded into the distance, but what could I do with him standing there, all "Ranger" flashes, notebook, and self-importance? I gave him my name, he lit a cigarette, and we waited in the gathering dark. I looked west, and the bridge changed from a dark, abstract outline to a big, simple piece of machinery as the lights came on.

9

THERE WAS JUST ENOUGH ROOM ON THE PATH FOR THE AMBULANCE. THE PARAMEDICS agreed with me and the ranger that the poor old bugger was dead. Then the cops arrived—plenty of space for them. They parked so that their headlights played over the scene, and after a fairly brief look around and collections of items such as the glasses and cap, they told the paramedics to take the corpse away. It all seemed a bit perfunctory to me, but it turned out that the senior constable knew old Stan, too, and he was satisfied with the "fell and hit head" explanation.

"And what were you doing in the gardens, Mr. Hardy?" he asked.

"Just taking a walk," I said.

"Funny time of day for a walk."

"I had things to think about, Constable."

"Satisfied" was the senior constable's middle name. He nodded, copied down the name and address from my driver's license, and told me that I should accompany them to the Woolloomooloo police station to sign my statement.

"I haven't made a statement."

The senior looked at his colleague, who read from his notebook, using his flashlight to read his notes. "I can take shorthand, Mr. Hardy. Your name is Cliff Hardy; I have your address as it appears on your driver's license. You were taking a walk in the Botanic Gardens at approximately four forty-five P.M., and you discovered the body of a man identified as Stan Livermore."

"That's right. I'm impressed."

"Just accompany us to the station, sir," the senior said. He turned to the ranger. "And you, too, sir, if you don't mind."

The ranger seemed to enjoy the ceremony; he spoke briefly into his walkie-talkie, and then we climbed into the back of the police car and drove slowly along the paths to the Victoria Lodge gate.

"I'm going to be late home," the ranger said.

I was playing the role of a solid, minding-my-own-business citizen. "Me, too," I said.

The constable was doing the driving; the senior was doing the investigating. "Did Stan have a family, d'you know?" he asked.

If it was a trap for me, it was too obvious. I said nothing and let the long pale gray shape of a warship docked opposite the Boy Charlton pool take my attention.

"Doubt it," the ranger said. "How long's this going to take?"

The senior shifted in his seat to let the pistol on his hip settle more comfortable. "Step on it, Charlie," he said. "The gentlemen want to get home for their tea."

The 'Loo police station is new and reasonably high-tech but rather undermanned. I noticed that the graffiti, a feature of the area, were starting to creep along nearby walls in its direction. The police wouldn't have the manpower to spare to scrub it off, so that station will probably look pretty much like the rest of the neighborhood soon. The shorthand expert typed up the ranger's statement, and he signed it and left. The constable then sat down at a computer terminal and put the microchips through their paces. I expected him to turn his professional attention to me after that, but the sergeant distracted him with some questions about something else. Then he couldn't find the right form; then he had to answer the phone a few times.

I sat in a too-bright room which had too few things to look at. I soon got bored by the community policing notices. There weren't any of the wanted posters—the ones with pictures of Neanderthal-faced men—that used to decorate police stations. The coffee from the automatic machine tasted like cocoa. I hate cocoa. I was impatient and restless, but I didn't want to occasion any suspicion. *Wouldn't an ordinary citizen be impatient and restless?* I thought. *Yes. Would he demand to see his lawyer or try to sneak out when the cop wasn't looking? No.* I sat and waited until the form was found and put in the typewriter and the sergeant went away and the phone stopped ringing. The magic fingers went to work again, and I was typed up, signed, and countersigned before you could say "police commissioner." I said that I was a real estate agent, but that was almost the only lie I told.

It was after eight o'clock when I left the police station, and as soon as I got out in the wind, I realized how cold and hungry I was. Also dry. It had been a good day for nonalcoholic resolutions, if not for much else. I had a light beer and a steak with salad and a half carafe of wine in a café in William Street.

The wine relaxed me and helped me to shift my attention from the disappeared and the dead to the living. Myself. I walked up to St. Peter's Lane and took a careful look around to see if anyone was lying in wait for me. I was in the mood. But not tonight, not yet at least. I checked my notebook for the address Ray Guthrie had given me and located it in the *Gregory's*. The Falcon had been sitting all day and was slow to start in the cold air. I let the motor run and turned on the heater. Darling Point. Maybe I should have gone home to change and shave. But if the good people of

Darling Point could put up with Rhino Jackson, who'd been known to spit on the pavement and worse, I couldn't see how they could object to me.

I drove down Darling Point Road, which bisects the peninsula. In some places structured like that, the rich people live off to the right and the poor to the left, or vice versa. In Darling Point the rich live off to the right *and* left. Ray had given me the name Nash; the address was a cul-de-sac that curled around from the main road and ended just short of the water. High fence, wide gate, bricked driveway; the front garden was so deep I couldn't see the house. There seemed to be a secondary driveway branching off the main one, and I guessed this was where the boating types backed their Mercs with catamarans attached down to the water. I gave it the once-over from the car, drove back three hundred feet and parked outside a big house from which cars had overflowed the three-car garage. There were no signs of a party inside—just too many cars per head. I put the .38 in my pocket and was all set to go when the rain started. I swore and dug the old oilskin slicker Cyn had given me as a birthday present out of the trunk. Cyn had thought I might take up yachting as a civilizing pursuit. Another disappointment.

I pulled up the hood and walked back along the road, squinting through the rain. The gates were open, but there was no activity. It was about three hours too early for the high rollers to show up; probably the hired muscle and the croupiers and the girls hadn't even arrived yet. The whole scene was tree-framed, shrub-bordered, and hedged. I slunk along under overhanging branches from the neighbor's garden to a point just a few feet from the Nash gate. A quick duck and dive, and I was through the gate and under cover again. I worked my way through ti tree and other foliage until I'd reached the point where the boat ramp branched off. I could see the house now: a two-story twenty-five-room splendido with too many pillars and steps. The big rooms had balconies; the smaller ones had window boxes.

The rain stopped, and I wiped my face with a piece of cloth I found in the pocket of the slicker. When I stuffed the rag back, I felt the hard metal of the gun, which was still in my jacket. I debated whether to transfer it to the slicker, but decided against; my policy is to make a gun as unavailable as possible. The fact that I'm still alive and haven't been shot more than a couple of times convinces me it's a good procedure.

I stayed close to the brick fence that separated Nash from his or her neighbor. I began to smell the sea before I'd got past the house. The ramp was bricked for some of the way, then made of tarred planks in the best nautical fashion. It was thirty feet wide, sloping easily down to a jetty on the left and straight into the water on the right. As well as a lane for boat trailers, there were metal rails for moving heavier craft on wagons and a space for vehicles to back up and turn in. A cluster of lights mounted high up over the ramp showed a number of small yachts tied up and the long, wide shape of the houseboat moored directly at the end of the jetty. It had a bulky superstructure which housed what they probably called staterooms. All very nice, Cyn would have loved it. Very civilized. But the lights were making the ramp and jetty look like the pitch at a night cricket match. No place for an interloper. Away to the right was a large, openfronted boatshed wrapped in shadow. I kept clear of the intersecting circles of light and picked my way past a barbecue pit and some garden furniture to the shed.

It rained some more while I waited. The tin roof of the shed amplified the sound but, true to the general standard of the place, didn't leak. I didn't explore the inner recesses of the shed more than I needed to. Boat gear is boat gear: oars, ropes, sails, tins of paint, and glue. When the rain stopped, other water noise took over: the slap of the sea against the piles of the jetty and the sides of the boats. There was also the creaking of timbers and a thrumming and slapping of the wind against ropes and furled sails. Another sound, which I couldn't identify at first, underlay all the others. It wasn't close enough to be disconcerting, but it was puzzling. A growling, scratching, rattling sound. I poked my head out of the shed and tried to see beyond the pools of light. Eventually I located the noise and its source: Somewhere on the other side of the boat ramp two dogs were chained up. Poor security; tying up the dogs when you were expecting strangers as guests was the right thing to do, but it had been done way too early.

The action started around midnight. Three cars came down the ramp, turned, and unloaded their passengers. I saw white shirts and fur coats and heard the click of high heels. A motor launch cruised up to the dock, and there was more movement and sound: Motors chugged; feet scraped on wood and metal. A few guys in red jackets appeared from nowhere and got busy. They turned on more lights over the jetty and on the houseboat itself. It was hard to judge its actual size from where I was, but it was big, long, wide, and high. The red coats started escorting people to the gangplank with elaborate courtesy. More arrivals by land and sea. I could hear music coming from the houseboat now and see people in clusters on the deck. The wind blew the rain clouds away, leaving a clear, starry sky beneath which the fun people got ready to play.

I counted forty-one people arriving, but I might have missed a few when my attention wandered. The red coats tied up and cast off for the launches, supported the tentative, valet-parked some cars, and generally kept things moving. One of them did less work than the others. His main job seemed to be okaying a member of each party. After forty minutes he rubbed his hands together and went on board, leaving the other two to stand on the jetty, smoke cigarettes, stamp their feet against the cold, and repel all boarders. There was no way to get aboard legitimately. Maybe I should have arrived in one of Ray's boats wearing a tux and with a woman on my arm. But I didn't have a tux or a woman.

Say what you like, army training can be useful. I fell back on it now instinctively. In a situation like this, training said: Attack head-on, or approach with stealth, or create a diversion. On the whole I prefer stealth, but not if it means getting wet on a cold winter night. Stealth failing, diversion is best, partly because it presents an intellectual challenge, but mostly because it cuts down the chances of getting shot through the head.

There are all sorts of handy things lying about in boatsheds. Rooting around in the semidark, I found a rescue kit, which included a flare pistol, plenty of petrol, a battery-powered loudspeaker, several spearguns—almost too many diversionary items. But I didn't want to start any fires or impale any red coats. I just wanted to see a man; no need for World War III. On the other hand, I'd been assaulted and had my name taken in vain in a court of law. And I was present at a highly illegal gaming operation; everyone around here was breaking the law. I looked the scene over again—yachts, houseboat, jetty, able-bodied guards, motor-cars parked along the upper reaches of the ramp—and the solution hit me.

I gathered up a long length of nylon cord and a couple of pulleys attached to screw clamps and left the boathouse, bent low and keeping to the shadows. I worked my way back to the ramp and along it behind the cars. There were seven of them: Volvos, BMWs, Saabs, and the like. The first six were parked pretty close together, but a red Porsche was a bit farther up the slope, as if it deserved a better view and a space of its own. Some of the cars were locked, but others had the keys hanging in the locks of the drivers' doors so the red coats could unpark them quickly and not keep the ladies and gentlemen waiting in the cold. The Porsche was open. I prized a brick out of the edge of the ramp, tied the end of the cord firmly around it, and set it carefully under the nearside front wheel of the Porsche. Then I opened the car and put the gearshift in neutral. I felt it roll an inch and come to rest on the two inches of brick that chocked the wheel.

I retreated toward the boatshed, paying out the nylon line. At two points I rigged up pulleys and passed the line through them. Tricky work with stiff, cold fingers and hard, unyielding nylon. The line was barely long enough; I had to crouch near the front of the shed, almost in one of the circles of light, and hope the guards didn't see me. I was sweating when I took up my position, and one leg was cramping from creeping and scuttling along. The guards were leaning against the jetty rail with their hands in their pockets. They didn't seem to be talking, but they weren't superalert. Bored, almost certainly, and probably tired.

I took a deep breath, surveyed the ground I'd have to cover to get to the jetty, and jerked the line. Nothing happened. I swore and pulled it again, putting some weight into the tug. I almost lost balance as the line slackened in my hands. I got ready to run. There was a moment's quiet and then a grinding crash as the freewheeling Porsche slammed into the back of the next car. That must have been one of the locked ones, with its alarm set. A bonus. The alarm started to whoop, and the guards shouted and ran toward the noise. I let them pass me and sprinted for the jetty. Any second now people would come out onto the houseboat's deck to see what the fuss was. But the natural place for them to look first was up, not down along the jetty. I broke the world record for running on planks, took the gangplank in two strides, and flattened myself against a wall of superstructure on the harbor side. I stood in the darkness, waiting for the confusion on the deck to reach a useful pitch. Clark Island was 260 feet away across the water. For no good reason I remembered the story Robert Hughes told about the place in *The Fatal Shore*. Lieutenant Clark used the island to grow vegetables, but the convicts rowed out and stole them. Sydney hasn't changed.

10

I THOUGHT I'D CAUSE SOME ALARM, STIR THE POSSUM, BUT WHAT I GOT WAS PANIC. Your illegal gambler these days must be a spineless type compared with the men and women in Perce Galea and Robin Askin's day. They'd talk to the cops, buy them drinks, swap racing tips, and go off to the lockup as if it were all part of the fun. Mind you, those were wide-open days, when MPs and magistrates winked and nodded so much they looked as if they all had palsy and tics.

As far as I could see from poking my head around the corner, this lot all wanted to abandon ship. I could hear persuading voices and protesting ones; voices were raised in anger, and threats were uttered. A motorboat came up in response to a hail from the houseboat. Two motorboat types in jeans and padded jackets came on board to back up a man in a dinner suit who was talking about money.

With the class of the company dropping, I felt safe in moving from my position along to a doorway that led inside the houseboat. Just inside the door were steps, going up and down. I went up a flight and came to what appeared to be a controls room. It featured a console with blinking lights, a navigator's desk, several office chairs, and windows giving a 360-degree view from a point about twenty feet above the water. I went down the steps and came to a short, narrow corridor with a door at the end. I held my shoulder against the door so it couldn't open and peered through a window in the shape of a porthole into the gambling room.

The place was about ten notches up from the one behind the coffee shop in Leichhardt. The bar was a thing of beauty—polished wood and steel, padded front, velvet-covered stools, all the trimmings. The socializing part of the room was lit by chandeliers; discreet, hooded lights hung over the tables and picked up the deep, rich colors in the paintings and tapestries on the walls. It should have been a scene of relaxed self-indulgence; instead it looked like a children's playground after a rainstorm. Chairs had been knocked over, and glasses of wine spilled, and cards and chips were scattered across the green baize surfaces. The barman and a couple of dealers had kept their places, but they were frozen, not touching any of the accoutrements in case the clients came back and protested that they'd been nobbled. A few last wisps of blue-gray smoke were drifting slowly toward a fan outlet. A classy joint, catering for the smoke-sensitive.

In the far corner of the room a blue velvet curtain hung over an opening. Another gambling room, perhaps, or executive space? I could get up adjacent to that area by opening the door at my shoulder. I had to move; a few people wandered back into the room, no doubt with stories of a crashed Porsche and a terrorist. They wouldn't find the brick immediately in the dark, but it wouldn't take too long. I eased back and opened the door. The man in the next stage of the corridor was surprised to see me, and he gave me a tiny advantage. I needed it because he was big and he wanted to stop me. He said something impolite and aimed a punch at my head, but I'd already moved the head and started a punch of my own. I got him low and hard. He grunted and sagged, and I hit him again on the back of the neck. He went down and fumbled in his jacket pocket. I used my knee to bang his head against the wall, and he stopped doing anything.

I stepped over him and took out my .38. I was pretty sure the guy on the floor hadn't been reaching for cigarettes. A door faced me at the end of the passage; it had a glass panel in it, and a face appeared there. I pointed the gun, and the face vanished. Another door was positioned to open into the space I'd seen from the porthole—the room behind the velvet curtain. *What the hell?* I thought. *I've flattened one of them, and I've got a gun. I'm tough. Someone'll have to talk to me.* I opened the door and stepped over the bulkhead.

The room was dark. Then, suddenly, it was flooded with light. I was half blinded, and things happened in a fast blur: A man rose up from the floor, pointed a camera at me, and took a series of pictures. Someone came from behind me and chopped the gun from my hand with a blow to my upper arm. I swung a punch with the other hand, and the photographer got a shot of that, too. The punch ended in the empty air, and I lost balance. It took only a good shove to deck me. I went down hard and felt solid boots hit me in the ribs on both sides, with near precision.

"Not the head."

I recognized the voice and turned my face toward it, but a hand ground my nose and chin down hard into the carpet. My arms were brought together behind my back, and I heard the snap of metal on metal.

"Jackson?" I mumbled into the carpet.

"Right first time, Hardy. Why is it you're always on the floor when we meet?"

I tried to scramble up, and a strong arm helped me by pulling on the handcuffs.

"Easy, Arch," Jackson said. "Don't mark him. And watch his feet. He's a tricky bugger."

A short, strongly built man pushed me back

against the wall. He grabbed a heavy swivel chair and used it to pin me there. I spit grit and fluff from my mouth, and with my vision more or less restored, I looked around the room. It was set up for very private card games: antique table with an expensive cloth, adjustable chairs, shaded light. There was a bar, smaller and less fancy than in the other room, but equipped for most tastes. The men in the room came in a variety of shapes and sizes: Rhino Jackson had changed a lot in the twenty-five years since he'd given me the quick count. He had been slight then, with quick, jerky movements. He was more like thickset the last time I'd seen him, a few years back, and since then he'd put on flesh uniformly from his neck down. The extra weight gave him a solid, immovable look. His tightly curled gingery hair was now almost entirely gray. I didn't recognize the photographer, who stood fiddling with the camera, or the guy Jackson had called Arch, the one who'd applied the handcuffs. The other man in the room, sitting at the card table with a cigar going, was Barry Tobin, formerly Detective Inspector Barry Tobin of the New South Wales police.

I'd had two run-ins with Tobin, both unpleasant. On a scale with my best friend at number one and worst enemy at number ten, Tobin would come in at around eight.

Tobin was gross, no other word for him. Not very tall, he was 90 percent blubber. The dark hair he'd been so vain about when he was young had gone, and the chief color in his face was ruby red. But unless the food and brandy had done to his brain what it had done to his body, he was smart.

He puffed on his cigar and tapped it carefully into an enamel ashtray on the table, taking care not to get ash on his three-piece suit. Still a dandy. "You were pretty easy to flatten, Hardy," he said.

I blinked. "Eye problem."

"I know, I know. Let's have a look at the pics."

The photographer handed him some Polaroids. Tobin held them toward the light. He laughed; the sound came out breathless and strangled. "Look at this, Rhino. He's blinking like Dicky Harrison. Remember Dicky, Rhino? That flasher we used to pick up and have some fun with? He used to blink like that. Always pissed, of course. Are you pissed, Cliff?"

I shook my head. Tobin always loved to hear himself talk.

"Can't have that," Tobin said. "We'll all have a drink in a minute."

Jackson opened the door and looked into the passage. "Christ, he did a good job on Kenny. Did you get that?"

The photographer nodded. "Bet your arse. Show you in a minute."

"What the hell is this?" I gave the chair a shove, but paleface shoved back.

"Easy, Arch," Jackson said. "Gently with him."

"You've met Arch before, Hardy. Realize that?"

I looked at Arch but didn't recognize him. "In church, maybe?" I said.

Tobin smiled. "Love a joke, don't you? No, he turned over your dump in Darlinghurst. Gave you a tap on the head, I understand."

"And pinched a photograph."

"That's right. Someone told us you had a picture with Rhino in it. Relic of the old days. We thought it'd help hook you if it went missing. Smart?"

I didn't reply. I could've said something about my damaged pizza, but I hadn't the heart. It *was* smart. I was hooked.

Jackson said, "Let's go up to the wheelhouse, Barry."

Tobin heaved himself from the chair.

"If you mean the ponced-up cockpit with the dials and switches, you'll never make it up the stairs," I said.

Tobin gave voice to another of his half-asphyxiated laughs. "I'll make it up, Hardy. Question is, will you make it down?"

The photographer went away; Arch moved the chair, and he, Jackson, Tobin, and I went out into the passage. Arch picked my gun up off the floor before we went. The man I'd knocked out was stirring but looking very sick. Tobin touched him on the shoulder. "Go and get a drink, Kenny. You did fine."

"Shit," Kenny said. "Do I get another go at him?"

"We'll see," Jackson said.

"Pity about the Porsche," I said.

Tobin paused before easing himself through the next doorway. "What?"

"I think I totaled a Porsche out there. Did some damage to a Merc, too."

Tobin's face flushed to the color of a ripe plum. His breath came in short spurts as he fought for control. "That's just a matter of money. That can be put right."

Arch prodded me forward, and we went through the door, along the passage and up the steps to the wheelhouse. We went slowly because Tobin took it one step at a time. I could hear sounds coming from the other side of the houseboat and from onshore: a couple of engines running, some urgent talk, and the clink of glasses.

"Sorry to spoil your party," I said.

Tobin stopped. Answering me gave him a chance to catch his breath and also to hear the sound he loved, that of his own voice. "Party's not spoiled, Cliff. Dismiss that thought from your mind. We've got very good people on the job out there. They'll smooth things over."

"What thoughts should I have on my mind? Apart from hoping your ticker gives out next step?"

"Oh, you might think about Beni Lenko and Didi Steller and the mystery witness. Yeah, try those thoughts on for size."

"That won't take long. I don't know any-thing about them."

Tobin didn't reply. We trooped through to the wheelhouse, which looked even more elaborate and digitalized when Jackson turned on the light. Then he pointed to a chair bolted to the floor in front of one of the devices with dials and switches. "Put him in the chair, Arch. Cuffs through the back. That's it. You can take a break now, mate. Call you if we need you."

Arch left. "Not a great talker, Arch," I said.

Tobin wheezed as he sat down out of kicking distance to my right. He pulled an ashtray toward him and shaped the end of his cigar. Jackson stood on the other side of the room. He fiddled with some switches. "Arch doesn't need to be a talker, Hardy, but you do. I asked you to think about Beni Lenko and Didi Steller."

"And I told you that all I know about them is what I read in the papers."

"Which was?"

"Come on, Tobin. What is this, the Quiz Kids?"

"Humor me."

"We're going to be in trouble if I need to wipe my nose."

Jackson wound a handle, and a window slid open. "I told you he was a smart-arse, Barry."

"Oh, I knew that. Do you mind telling me what the fuck you're doing?"

"The smoke," Jackson said.

"Close it! I like to fill a room with smoke. Hardy?"

I sighed. "Didi Steller hired Lenko to hit her rich husband. Lenko did a good job. Overcome with remorse, Didi killed herself with sleeping pills. Beni only got half his fee and was dumb enough to talk about it. So he got charged with murder."

Tobin nodded. "Mistrial, first up."

"Pity," I said.

"Especially for you," Jackson said.

"That's what I was coming to see you about, Rhino. I understand my name got mentioned by someone the cops are keeping under wraps. And you couldn't be found to throw any light on the matter."

"Did you help to set up the hit?" Tobin said.

"Me? Set up a hit? In your case I might think about it. Otherwise, no."

Tobin and Jackson exchanged a satisfied look, which puzzled me.

"Good," Tobin said.

"Did I say something right? How about Rhino saying something?"

"Like what?" Jackson coughed on the words. He really didn't like the smoke. I didn't care for it too much myself, but there was always the chance that Tobin might smoke himself to death right there and then.

"You knew Lenko pretty well. I wouldn't be surprised if you put him away a time or two. And then you probably saw him again when you went inside yourself."

"Just for interest," Tobin said, "have you ever been inside, Hardy?"

"Remand. Long Bay. Six weeks. About one percent of what you'll get one of these days."

"I doubt it," Tobin said.

There was a quiet knock at the door. Jackson opened it, and the photographer came in carrying a video camera. "Top stuff," he said.

Tobin beckoned him across. The photographer pressed a button on the camera, and they put their heads close together to watch the small screen. Tobin's wheezy chuckle would have gone over well in the tunnel of horrors. He waved to Jackson, who shook his head. "Just so long as it's what we need."

"Don't be a spoilsport, Rhino," Tobin said. When Jackson didn't react, he jerked his thumb at me. "Show him how he looks in action."

The photographer brought the camera across and pressed the button. I saw myself in the corridor just after I'd come through the door. The camera must have been mounted high; it caught Kenny's reaction, and I saw I'd made a mistake when I thought I'd got him by surprise. He was more than ready. So ready that he telegraphed and slowed his punch, making it easy for me. Still, I looked pretty good in there, and I'm sure the coup de grace wasn't in the script.

"Nice bit of work with the knee," Tobin said.

I nodded. "I thought so at the time. I see it a

bit differently now. I don't think Kenny was expecting the knee."

Tobin ground out his cigar butt. "Maybe not, but you can't always plan things down to the last detail. It wouldn't be Kenny's first king hit. Now"—he reached into his pocket and took out the Polaroids—"you don't look quite so good in these."

The photographer showed me the pictures; he strayed closer than he should have. I looked —a man with a crazed look in his face was blinking and waving a gun around that looked to be the size of a howitzer, good angle—but I didn't give the photographs my full attention. When I was sure he was in range, I swung my right foot hard into the photographer's knee. He screamed, dropped the photographs, and went down hard, whimpering. He scrambled up and hobbled toward me with the video camera held high. Jackson sprang forward, snatched the camera with one hand, and gave the photographer a rabbit punch with the other. He went down again.

"It's not your night, sport," I said.

Jackson put the camera and pictures on the navigation desk and snapped his fingers at the man on the floor. "Out," he said. "Go and have a drink."

I grinned. "With Kenny."

The photographer shot me an evil look and limped out. Tobin lit another cigar. His amused calm worried me more than Jackson's nervous energy. I looked around as best I could, immobilized as I was in the chair. There was nothing much to see; we were twenty feet above the water; the lights of Darling Point looked a million miles away.

Tobin puffed his cigar. "Tight spot, Cliff."

"I admit I'm puzzled . . . Barry."

"What about scared?"

"Should I be? You haven't hurt me yet. I'd say I was winning, head to head."

"You don't know what the game is. Let's hear it, Rhino."

Jackson fiddled with the switches again, and I heard my voice loud and clear: "Me? Set up a hit? In your case I might think about it. . . ." Jackson hit a button and the tape stopped. He fiddled some more, and I heard myself say, "Lenko did a good job. . . ."

11

TOBIN COULDN'T RESIST TELLING ME ALL ABOUT IT. HOW HE'D HELPED SET UP THE HIT with Lenko; how Jackson had used my name when dealing on the telephone with Prue Harper. Harper was a prostitute Didi Steller used to mix with for the thrill of being on the edge of the demimonde. Everything went wrong when Didi suicided and Lenko started talking.

"Couldn't have anticipated that." Tobin couldn't talk or do anything for long without a drink. He'd fished out a bottle of scotch and was on his second snort. Jackson was nursing one. They hadn't offered me any.

"I don't know," I said. "You must have known that Didi was unstable and Beni was dumb. I'd say you screwed up, Barry. Your name came up, did it? I expect Prue Harper'd know you."

Tobin smiled. "We took out a bit of insurance there by throwing your name into the pool, as it were."

I began to get an inkling of what was going on then. The photographs, the film, the kid-glove treatment. It smelled of a setup, and from what I knew about Tobin, the details would be nasty. "Did you have a hand in this hearing business? The review of my license?"

Tobin nodded. "I've still got a few friends on the force. But don't worry, Hardy, you won't have to attend any hearing."

Jackson snickered behind me.

"Don't you see it?" Tobin said. "You're going to kill poor little Prue."

I stared at him. A cramp had started in my arms and was sending a sharp pain up into my shoulders when I moved. I worked my wrists up and down in the few inches of free play available. The cramp got worse, and I winced. "You're crazy. I'm not killing anybody."

Jackson worked the controls of his tape recorder again, and my voice said, ". . . know Prue Harper."

"As it happens," Tobin said, "you don't know her. But by the time the experts get through with this tape it'll sound as if you do. In fact, it'll sound as if you know everything and have been a very bad boy."

"Bullshit. They can spot doctored tapes."

"Not always. You'd be amazed at some of the advances in that field in recent times. Especially in the States." Tobin waved his cigar. "And I've got a few connections there, too."

"I can't understand why you left the force," I said. "I know all about Rhino. He got caught. But you're so smart, Barry. What went wrong?"

Tobin's face took on the plum color again. He gulped his drink and poured some more. I'd found the soft spot, but I doubted it could do me any good. "You're history, Hardy. Prue Harper's going to be found dead, and these pictures and the tape are going to support the view that you killed her. And you're not going to be in a position to contradict that view, if you follow me."

I shook my head. "Fantasy."

Tobin smiled. "You're not going to tell us you never killed anybody?"

It wasn't a subject I thought a lot about. I'd killed plenty of men in Malaya, but that had been in war, which was different, or so they told you and so you told yourself. As a civilian I'd killed two men. One had been pointing a loaded gun at the man standing next to me, and the other, still worse, had been all set up to shoot me.

Jackson said, "We've got your gun, Cliff."

"Means nothing."

Tobin leaned forward from where he was sitting. He kept out of kicking range, but I could smell the tobacco and whiskey fumes like a rich, sickly breeze. He was still agitated and angry. "They'll call your mate Parker. And he'll have to admit that you questioned him about the witness protection program. A good barrister'll get that out of him and no more."

Jackson was getting into the spirit of it as well. He finished his drink, and Tobin poured him another, a big one. "And Lou Campisi'll say you asked him about where to find me. Of course, he won't mention the boat."

"Was that a setup, too?"

"Let's say we studied up on you." Tobin was calming down. He sucked in air, and the flush in his swollen, distended face receded. "Learned your habits. You were a sitting duck for something like this, Hardy. Parker aside, you're not popular with the force. And inside the force *he's* not exactly a pinup boy. I don't think you've got too many friends, anywhere you look."

"I've got a few in the press."

"Wankers," Tobin said. "And a dead private eye's not much of a story. They're *supposed* to be dead or in jail. Didn't I read a survey on the professions somewhere? Rating them in public esteem? I don't think private detective even got a mention. I know that journalists were near the bottom."

"They'd rate above bent cops."

"Let's get on with it, Barry," Jackson said.

I needed time. A cold fear was spreading through me, partly because time had suddenly become so valuable. And not because I had any idea of what to do with it. I just wanted the time. "What about Lenko? How does he fit into all this?"

"Fuck him," Jackson said.

Tobin nodded. "This is a housekeeping exercise, you might say. Also something of an experiment."

I seized on that as something to hold back the second hand. "Experiment?"

"Sure. If it works the way we think it will, this tape thing has endless possibilities."

"You're dreaming."

"That's right, Hardy." Tobin had regained his cool and was motormouthing again. "You have to dream to get anywhere. Look at you— a cut-rate private eye. All you've done in the past ten years is pay off a bit of your mortgage. The opportunities you must've let slip by . . ."

"Limitless," I said. For a moment I wondered whether there was any chance of convincing them I'd do a deal. But I rejected the idea; dirty deals were Tobin and Jackson's bread and butter. They'd spot a faker as soon as he opened his mouth. I could think of only one other tack to take. "I can see how this little plot puts you in the clear, Barry. But I can't see so much in it for Rhino." I moved as much of my body as I could to get a good straight view of Jackson, who was still playing with switches. He didn't even look at me.

"Rhino'll have to go away for a while," Tobin said. "Somewhere nice. But the heat'll go out of this pretty soon, and he'll be able to come back."

I wasn't just sitting there passively all this time. I was moving my wrists and arms, trying to work some slack, wondering whether I could slip my hands out of the jacket and oil-skin and through the cuffs. No chance. Arch knew what he was doing when he put them on. He was probably an ex-copper, too. The back of the chair didn't feel too strong, but there was no chance of breaking it with two able-bodied men watching me. If I'd been Houdini, I'd have had a picklock under my thumbnail and the joke would be on them. But I can't even do card tricks. All I could do was talk. "I still think you're crazy trying on something like this. Too complicated. This new corruption committee they've got could hear little stories."

This time Jackson did look at me, but only to laugh. "That committee'll hear what the right people want it to hear. And in the end it'll do what it's told. Right, Barry?"

Tobin was about to nod when I scored my first real hit on him. "Hope you're getting all this on tape, Rhino."

Tobin's eyes popped. Veins stood out in his forehead as he turned to look at Jackson. "You'd better have turned that fucking thing off—"

Jackson looked flustered. "It's okay, Barry. I can wipe it. I—"

"He's taking out some insurance of his own, Bazza," I said.

"Shut up, Hardy," Tobin growled. "Rhino, I—"

"What the hell's that?" As intent as he was on the confrontation with Tobin, Jackson couldn't ignore the noise outside. I heard shouts and a splash, and then the blue, blinking light of a police beacon flashed in the window. "Shit," Jackson said, "there's some fuckin' D and a couple of uniforms down there."

That was enough encouragement for me. I slung myself out of the chair as far as I could, which wasn't far but enough to get a kick at the table Tobin was sitting at. His ashtray and glass went flying through the air, and I nearly tore every ligament in my arms when I wrenched at the back of the chair, trying to pull the handcuffs clear. I broke the plastic part away from the metal part and was almost loose. Tobin roared something, and I swung around, kicking at him, shouting myself, and trying to create as much uproar as I could. I swung back the other way and was free, apart from having my arms pinned behind me, being attached to a small section of chair, and having cramps in my legs. I bullocked my way across the cockpit and butted Rhino Jackson in the midsection. He was holding a gun at the time, which I hadn't known or I mightn't have done it. The gun went off, and the noise in the confined space was like a rocket launch. A window exploded.

After that, time and certain other things became very confused. Maybe there was an answering shot from a nervous trigger finger below, maybe not. Both Jackson and Tobin made for the door and fought to get through it and down the steps. I followed, although I didn't know why. I was slow and clumsy. Jackson turned and fired at me, but I was falling downstairs at the time, and he missed. When I hit the bottom, I struggled up and out through the open door onto the back part of the deck where I'd hidden when I first came aboard.

I fell again, unable to grab at any support. I felt my head hit something hard and warm blood flow down into my right eye. It would've been a perfect moment to shoot me. But no one did. I was lying on the hard, wooden deck with my blood flowing, my arms sending up pain messages to my brain, and only one eye working. From this low vantage point, I saw a uniformed policeman present himself in front of Jackson, who had somehow got ahead of Tobin and shout at both of them to stop where they were. Tobin shoved Jackson forward, and the cop shot him in the chest. Moving with an agility I could hardly believe, Tobin swung his legs over the side. The cop was standing stockstill, shocked at what he'd done. I expected to hear a splash, but instead there was the roar of an engine firing and a churning noise as a boat took off across the water, away from flying bullets and falling bodies and flowing blood.

12

"YOU MUST BE HARDY. IS THAT RIGHT?"

The big man bending over me was breathing heavily and sweating. I'd seen him before —in Arundel Street in the company of the widowed Mrs. Glover and her unpleasant son, Clive.

I wriggled up into a sitting position. I had an aching head, a closing eye, and pain almost everywhere. "And you must be Detective Sergeant Meredith. I'm very pleased to see you."

"Yeah, I bet you are. Could you tell me what the hell's going on here? I came looking for you and—"

"For me? Why?"

"You left your name at the morgue. I wanted to know why you were interested in Glover. Then I saw the sheet from the Woolloomooloo station that you were on the scene when another guy died, and in sight of the bridge. We have to talk, Hardy."

"Sure. But how did you know to come here?"

"I put out a marker on your car. A cruiser spotted it up the road and called in. We're pretty well organized these days."

The flashing blue light had been turned off, but there was still a lot of commotion on and around the jetty and on the houseboat. The sorts of protesting voices that I'd heard before were being raised again, and the cops were talking in their quiet, emotionless way. I'd really spoiled some folks' night. Meredith took a look over my shoulder at the handcuffs.

"Can you locate a guy named Arch?" I said. "He should have the key to these bloody things. How come you piled in like this? I thought you just wanted a chat."

"If you mean Arch Bailey, we've got him in custody. He's wanted. That's what I mean. I arrived and found all these bloody crims swarming around—Bailey, Fred Murdoch, Sammy Camarella. Couple of them ponced up in red jackets like they were in Las Vegas. All on the wanted list. I called in for support. What's going on, Hardy?"

I grinned at him. "You just raided Barry Tobin's gambling boat. You've probably got the odd magistrate and MP in chains down there."

"Shit." Meredith pushed his lank fair hair back from his eyes. He was younger than I'd thought, at least ten years younger than I. His bulk had misled me. In the dim light he looked almost boyish. "Who cares?" he said. "Those old pricks have had it coming for years. Their protection's just about run out."

"Good," I said. I jiggled the short chain on the cuffs. "Arch?"

Meredith's eyes went suddenly shrewd. "Still, I could be in the shit over this. You wouldn't have anything else to tell me, would you, Hardy?"

"A lot, on this and the bridge business. But first you should send someone up to get a tape from the wheelhouse."

"The what?"

"Up there!" I jerked my head to indicate the direction, and then I saw Rhino Jackson. Two men, one in uniform, one in a dinner suit, were bending over him in attitudes that suggested he was a lost cause. Meredith gave urgent commands to a couple of the cops, and one returned with a key to the handcuffs. When I was free, I moved across to where Jackson lay. They'd put a blanket over the lower part of his body. The policeman who had shot him was young, pale-faced, and scared. He looked up and saw me.

"You saw it, didn't you? You saw what happened."

"Yes," I said. "I saw it. It wasn't your fault. Don't worry, son." I looked at the man in the dinner suit.

"I'm a doctor," he said. "I'm afraid he hasn't

got very long. The bullet must have hit something vital."

The young cop turned away, and I bent over Jackson. His eyes opened. "Hardy?" he whispered.

"Rhino."

"Tobin." The voice was a harsh whisper with no force behind it. "Get Tobin . . . kill Prue Harper."

"Tobin's going to kill her?"

"Has to. She knows . . ."

"Where is she?"

Meredith was beside me now. "What's this?" he said.

"Shush. Where is she, Rhino?"

A trickle of blood came from Jackson's mouth, and his eyes closed.

"He's going," the doctor said.

Jackson's lips pursed as if he were about to spit. I bent my head down. I could feel his breath, the faintest, sour-smelling whisper, on my face. "Budget . . ."

"Budget . . ." I repeated.

The bloodless lips trembled, pursed, relaxed, then firmed up again. "Back . . . packer."

"I know it," Meredith said. "Budget Backpacker. Victoria Street. The Cross. Hardy—"

"I think he's gone," the doctor said. He checked Jackson's pulse, shook his head, and pulled the blanket up over the white, still face with the dark trickle running from the slack mouth.

The young cop jammed his hands in his pockets and stood like an actor onstage who didn't know his next line. Meredith touched his shoulder. "Go and have a cigarette, Constable."

"I don't smoke, sir."

"Then go and have a bloody drink."

"I don't . . ."

He was almost in shock. I steered him along the deck. "There must be a kitchen in this boat somewhere. You can probably get a cup of coffee or something. Hang on, son. You'll be all right."

"Hardy!"

I turned to see Meredith beckoning me. He was holding a .38 Smith & Wesson that looked very like mine, also a tape cassette and the Polaroid photographs of me in blinking, blundering action. I approached him and held out my hand for the gun.

"Don't make me laugh," he said. "You're a menace."

"This was all a setup, Meredith. It's not the way it looks. But I'll tell you one thing: Barry Tobin's on his way to kill someone who's supposed to be safe under a witness protection program."

"I don't understand any of this. What?"

"There really isn't time to explain. A lot of it's on that tape. If we had time, you could call Frank Parker and he'd vouch for me, but I reckon you should take a punt. You believe in the witness protection program, don't you?"

"Of course."

"Then you'd better get to the Budget Back-packer before Tobin does, or witness protection'll have about as much credibility as the weather bureau."

Maybe it was because Meredith was young, maybe because he had imagination, maybe it was a rebellious streak, but he broke a lot of rules in getting himself, me, and one of the constables away from the shambles on the *Pavarotti* in double-quick time. I sat in the backseat of the speeding police car, cleaning myself up with bunches of tissues from the box Meredith handed me.

"You're a mess," Meredith said.

"So would you be if you had to do the sorts of things I have to do."

"You must tell me about it sometime. Right now I could do with some background on what we're getting into now."

I filled him in as best I could, remembering scraps as I went along and backtracking to fit them into the story.

"Are you following this, Constable Moody?" Meredith said to the driver.

"No, sir." Moody's voice had the harsh note characteristic of the city Aboriginal. I noticed that his hands and the back of his neck were brown. He drove with the economy and decisiveness of a professional.

"Me neither."

"You would if you heard the tape. Have you got it safe?"

Meredith patted his breast pocket. "Yep. You saying Barry Tobin set up the hit?"

"Yes. And I don't think it's the only one he set up. This Prue Harper apparently knows a bit about it, so Jackson said."

Meredith's big head nodded. His hair was longish at the back, straggling over his ears and collar. My grandma used to say that untidiness was a sign of honesty. It meant you weren't always out to make the right impression. On that score Meredith was honest. "A dying declaration," he said. "Pity we haven't got it on tape."

"Victoria Street, sir," the driver said.

We'd approached from the Potts Point end of the street, leaving the water below and behind us. There was no telling what route Tobin would take and no knowing whether he'd get there before us or after. I shrugged out of the oilskin, which was making me hot, and finished dabbing at my cuts and abrasions. The aches in my arms and legs would have to take care of themselves. I remembered the last time I'd seen Tobin in action, when he was blasting away with a shotgun, and I suddenly felt vulnerable and exposed.

"There it is. Pull over." Meredith sounded edgy too. He pointed through the windshield at the big three-story terrace house which had a neon sign over the gate: BUDGET BACKPACKER. "Christ knows how they run these things,"

Meredith said. "Do they just deposit the protected witness somewhere they consider safe
and leave it at that? Or do they keep a watch?"

"Haven't you been briefed?" I said.

Meredith glanced at the driver who was sitting rigidly, with his hands on the steering
wheel. "I was busy," he said. "Let's take a look.
You'd better check your weapon, Constable
Moody, but for God's sake don't use it unless
you have to."

"What about my weapon?" I said.

"What about it?"

"Tobin's got more reason to kill me than you
or Moody. He might think I've got the tape."

Meredith stared ahead at the street and
didn't reply. It was about two in the morning
and fairly quiet. Not that it's ever completely
quiet at the Cross. There were people in the
street, drifting along, getting close to the end
of their day. The street was lined with cars,
some of them, the Falcon and Holden station
wagons mostly, the vehicles that Backpackers
would try to sell the following day. There were
cars with resident stickers and others belong-
ing to the people who came to the Cross for
alcohol, food, and sex or just to look.

Moody had checked his pistol and returned
it to the holster. "I know Prue Harper, sir," he
said.

"Do you?" Meredith said. "That helps."

"Do you want me to go in and bring her out,
sir?"

Meredith opened his door. "It's not a bad idea. Hardy, you stay here."

I opened my door. "Not without my gun."

Meredith hesitated. We were parked about 150 feet from the gate of the house. The street was well lit, and the pavement, looking back toward Darlinghurst Road, was like a shooting gallery.

Meredith shook his head. "If you see anything, Hardy, turn on the siren. Show him how it works, Constable."

Moody showed me the switch. I nodded. "Great. I'll tackle him while he's suffering temporary blindness and hearing loss."

"Look," Meredith said, "Tobin won't know that Jackson told us anything. He'll be counting on confusion and delay. It's very unlikely that he'll show. We'll go in and get the woman. That's it."

"There's a lane at the back," Moody said. "Bound to be another way in."

"Shit," Meredith said. "All right, Hardy, here's your bloody gun. You stay here. I'll go around the back and check it. Then the constable and I'll go in the front door. Before sunrise, I hope."

Meredith retreated around the nearest corner. I sat in the passenger seat next to Moody. I was tense; he seemed relaxed. "How d'you come to know Prue Harper?" I said.

Moody stared ahead. "I know lots of people."

"What's she like?"

"Foolish," he said.

A clutch of people came down the street: three large blond young men and a couple of women of the same stamp. They separated. A couple went into the house we were watching; the others crossed the road to the Hotel California: BACKPACKERS WELCOME.

"Lucky buggers," Moody said. "Where do you reckon they're from?"

I shrugged. "Germany, Sweden."

"Wouldn't mind going there myself." Suddenly he leaned forward. I tried to see where he was looking.

"What?" I said.

"Look there." He pointed. "The Tarago."

A large van was moving slowly toward us. I couldn't see the driver or anyone else in the van, but Moody could. He gave me a shove which hurt one of the ribs Arch had kicked. "The driver's checking the place out. Get down!"

We slumped down, and the van cruised past. Moody sneaked a look in the rearview mirror.

"What's it doing?"

"Stopping," he said. "Two guys getting out. Skinny bloke and a fat one, real fat. That him?"

"Could be."

"They're going around the back."

"Can't sit here," I said. I opened my door and eased out, keeping low. The street was empty now; Moody ran for the corner, and I limped after him. The street we turned into was narrow and dark. I could just glimpse the entry to a lane which ran behind the terrace houses fronting Victoria Street. Moody disappeared into the lane. I followed him after looking cautiously around the corner first. I saw shapes moving ahead, darting from one side of the lane to the other. I moved ahead slowly, pressing back against a brick wall.

Two shots, clean and sharp like whipcracks, sounded in quick succession. Then I heard Meredith shout, "Stop! Police!"

A third shot, with a heavier note, boomed out, and the lane was suddenly full of echoes and swearing and the sounds of running feet. A figure loomed up in front of me, running fast. Too tall to be Moody, too slight for Meredith. I stepped out and tried to raise my gun, but he arrived too soon. Too soon for him as well. He swung something short and stubby at me; I ducked under the swing and dived forward, hitting about knee-high and sending him thumping hard onto the ground, headfirst. There was a roar as the shotgun he had been carrying hit the brick wall and went off. Pellets flicked around, ricocheting from the bricks and roadway. They missed me. He didn't move.

I got up and peered through the gunsmoke, but I couldn't see anything. I'd dropped my gun. I bent over, feeling for it as much as looking. Suddenly Tobin was there—wide as a house with his breath coming in wheezy gasps and his chest heaving. He pointed a pistol at me, and I froze.

"Fuck you, Hardy. Fuck you . . ."

I could see him getting up the will to shoot me, and I couldn't move or speak. The shotgun was on the road, but it was a mile away. Tobin shuffled forward, making sure. . . .

I waited for the explosion, but instead I heard a sound no louder than a whisper. Moody rose up from the shadows and chopped the pistol from Tobin's grasp with a blow that cracked the bones in Tobin's hand. Moody grabbed Tobin's arm and jerked it up behind him. Tobin resisted, straining to use his bulk against the lighter man. As I moved forward to help, a car swung into the lane and hit us with its headlights. Moody rammed his gun into Tobin's ear.

"Give it up!"

Tobin jerked his head around and saw the dark, intense face close to his own. "You black cunt! You fuckin' boong . . ."

Moody jammed his gun in harder. "Sticks and stones, *gubbah*," he said. "Sticks and stones."

PART
TWO

PART
TWO

13

HAVING MY BACON SAVED TWICE IN THE ONE NIGHT BY POLICEMEN WAS AN UNUSUAL
experience. I thanked and complimented
Moody, but there was no way to communicate
with Meredith. Barry Tobin had shot him
twice, in the chest and in the leg, and while I
was being interviewed, cross-examined, and
warned, Meredith was in St. Vincents fighting
for his life.

Eventually, with the help of Frank Parker, I
got things sorted out. The police had the tape
and the film and the photographs and a statement from me which probably didn't make a
lot of sense—it was 3:00 A.M., and I'd suffered a
fair amount of personal abuse—but laid em-
phasis on my innocence. With my battered
head, torn pants, and shotgun pellet–ripped
jacket, I had credibility as the victim of a con-

spiracy. Parker assured me that if I had to appear in the magistrate's court, it would be only to receive an apology. I would have been feeling more or less cheerful if it hadn't been for Meredith.

"He's pretty tough," Parker said. "Used to play hockey, they tell me." Frank was driving me home. It was three forty-five. His wife wouldn't be happy at my keeping her man working so late, but as my former tenant she knew my erratic habits.

I was so tired that forming words felt like building a brick wall, but after all the trouble Parker had gone to, it would have been bad form just to nod off there in the car. "Is hockey a game for tough guys?"

"Ice hockey, in Canada."

"Oh. Yeah. I'm with you." I'd seen North American hockey games on TV. I remembered watching one with Helen Broadway. She called it an abattoir on ice, which was about right.

Frank turned into Glebe Point Road. Tired as I was, I still instinctively helped him to drive the car, checked the oncoming traffic, and mentally changed down. Even crazier in this instance, because Frank's car was an automatic. Parker glanced at me as I twitched in the passenger seat. "Meredith's a bright man. Did a postgraduate degree in criminology at McGill University. He's a bit of a hothead, but he had—he's got a bright future."

I nodded and wished I hadn't. Inside my

head little popping noises were getting louder and louder. I could hardly hear what Frank was saying, and my own voice sounded thin and far off. "He saved my arse back there on the houseboat. That's for sure."

"Care to tell me how he came to be there?"

"Missing persons case," I said. "We're working on parallel lines. I mean, our lines of inquiry intersected. . . . Shit, Frank, I don't know what I'm saying."

Parker pulled up outside my house. "It's all right. I'll have Meredith's number two give you a ring. Bloke named Wren, Ralph Wren. He's okay."

"Make it the day after tomorrow," I said. "I'm knackered."

"Right. Need a hand?"

I opened the car door and almost fell out onto the pavement. Parker moved as if to get out of his seat, but I shook my fist at him. "I'm okay, Frank. Thanks for everything. Go home to Hilde. I'm okay. I'll try to see Meredith tomorrow."

Parker reached over and closed the door. The window had been open because I'd wanted the cold air on my flushed face. "Get some sleep, Cliff," he said, "and don't do anything on your case until you talk to Wren."

I saluted and lurched toward the front gate. I didn't have my gun or my oilskin anymore. I'd lost some brain cells and several inches of skin from various parts of my anatomy. But I had my key. I scratched and scraped until I got it in the lock and turned it. I was thinking of a hot bath. Maybe a hot drink as well. Rum and hot water. It'd probably knock me out and I'd drown in the bath. But the tub leaked, and if I had a bath, I'd have to mop up the water in the morning. I couldn't face that. Not a wet mop! Not ever again! I went into the musty, closed-all-day, no fun being had here–smelling house, turning on lights and trying to feel human.

The daybed in the sitting room beckoned me, but I made it to the kitchen and a tap. I washed my face at the sink and dried it on a dishcloth which smelled of cat food. Where was the cat? I looked around and called out him in a voice I hardly recognized. If I'd been a cat, I wouldn't have come to that voice. The cat didn't. I drank two cups of water, staggered through to the daybed, and lay down. I jerked up like a marionette to pull off my jacket and thought about turning off the lights. Thought about it, didn't do it. I passed out into a black and gray zone of sonar booms, drifting smoke, and bright flashing lights that made sounds like the little ten-for-a-penny Tom Thumb firecrackers I used to let off when I was a kid.

When I woke up, somewhere around 8:00 A.M., I knew I should have had the bath, plus a massage and a long sleep in a soft, warm bed. The daybed is a hard, unyielding structure that Helen accused me of installing to deter casual stopover visitors. Maybe she was right; she often was. I levered myself off the thing and, bent over like a bell ringer, moved toward the shower, hoping the hot water would help me straighten up. In the kitchen the cat confronted me and demanded that I straighten up sooner, preferably with a can opener in my hand. I told it to get lost and went through to the cold, drafty bathroom to get myself some steam.

It took about an hour—steam, coffee with rum, toast with honey, and a feeding of the cat —but eventually I felt better. Well enough, anyway, to sit down by the telephone and think about what to do next. It would have been nice just to sit there with my second rum-laced coffee and drift for a while. Let things sort themselves out in my mind, wait for connections. Instead I rang Louise Madden in Leura and asked when I could see her.

"Why?" she said.

"To talk. I might be on to something, but I need to talk to you."

"Why can't we talk now? We *are* talking now."

"I think my phone might be tapped. Nothing to do with this matter, but . . ."

"My, my. You *are* the man of mystery, aren't you? I'm working on a garden in Castlecrag today. That any good to you?"

It was; it was even a connection of a kind. I arranged to meet her at the address in Castlecrag in midafternoon. My next call was to Paul Guthrie at Northbridge. Castlecrag and

Northbridge, not bad. It could just have easily been Northbridge and Chipping Norton. I told Guthrie that the information Ray had given me had been very helpful and that I needed Ray's help again.

"You sound a bit shaky," Guthrie said.

"I'm fine. I'd like to see Ray. Where would I find him, say, later this afternoon?"

"Right here if you want. You just have to ask, Cliff."

I didn't feel good about it. Old fathers have no right to command the movements of their young sons, but the Guthries were a close-knit family, almost sharing the same mind. So perhaps it wasn't too bad. I said I'd be at the Northbridge house around six, and Paul Guthrie assured me his son would be there. That left me with about six hours to fill and two things to do: recover my car and visit, if that was possible, Detective Sergeant Meredith in St. Vincents Hospital.

I had the car keys in my jacket pocket. I walked up Glebe Point Road past the cafés and bookshops and caught a cab just this side of Parramatta Road. In Darling Point I found the Falcon just as I'd left it except that there was a flyer under the wiper. "Protect your Independence," it read. "Your Independent local member is under threat from the conservative government's plan to change the composition of the Parliament. Write to me. Write to the premier." I crumpled up the paper and was about to drop it into one of the big plastic garbage bins that help keep Darling Point clean when I took a good look at the neighborhood. I thought the "local Independent member" had a right to be concerned: The big white houses with their gardens and driveways and high walls smacked of conformity rather than independence. I unfolded the notice and tucked it into into a wrought iron gate, just above the security lock.

Hospital visits might be some people's idea of a kick, but not mine. For me, there's always too much waiting about, too many starched white uniforms, and too much of a feeling that the walls are saying, "You're on your feet now, but you could be on a stretcher tomorrow."

I gave my name at the desk and after seeing two nurses and a policeman—it's standard procedure to have a cop on duty after a cop has been shot; why I'm not sure—I was allowed to see Meredith.

"He's out of intensive care," the ward nurse who was escorting me to Meredith's room said. "He's such a strong man! He responded to everything the doctors did."

"You sound surprised, Sister. Do most intensive care patients die?"

She looked as if she had things to say on the subject but thought better of it. "Yes, eventually, Mr. Hardy. We all do. Even doctors. He's in here." She pushed open a door. "Five minutes."

"And no arm wrestling," I said. I can't help it, hospitals and nurses affect me that way.

I went into the room, which was no bigger than it needed to be for the bed and a lot of medical equipment. It smelled of sterile plastic and glass and detergent. I could barely recognize Meredith for tubes and wires running in and out of his face and body. The tubes and wires were hooked up to drips and monitoring devices; lights were blinking on the equipment, and blips were dancing across green screens.

"Looks like they're about to launch you into outer space," I said.

Meredith face twitched. A smile, maybe. "G'day, Hardy."

"Sorry about all this. What're they telling you?"

"Bugger all, but I reckon I'll be all right. Felt worse after some hockey games."

"Yeah, I can imagine."

"Are you talking about the bullet or the hockey?"

"Never played ice hockey. I got a bullet in the leg once. Hurt like hell and still twinges sometimes. Well, I just wanted to look in. Didn't think you'd be in real trouble. What caliber was Tobin's gun? Nothing you couldn't handle?"

Again the twitch, the possible smile. A couple of sentences had tired him.

"That Moody did all right," he whispered.

"Bloody tremendous. Well, I don't want to

keep you here any longer than necessary, so I'll—"

"Hardy."

"Don't talk, Meredith. You're tough, but don't push your luck. It'll keep."

"Bridge . . . foundry . . . Samuels an' . . . Booth . . . missing. I think . . ."

I could hear the nurse's footsteps coming down the hall, and I was looking for somewhere to pat him without touching a piece of medical intervention. I touched his broad, meaty shoulder. "Take it easy, Sergeant. I know what you're talking about. Just concentrate on getting better."

"Don't—"

"Don't worry. Is there anything you want?"

Meredith's hard gray eyes were clouding over with fatigue. A slight movement might have been a shake of the head. I patted his shoulder again and retreated to the door, which opened as I got there.

"I was just coming to ask you to leave, Mr. Hardy," the nurse said.

"That's okay, Sister," I said. "In a hospital being asked to leave is okay. Ask me to stay and I'd worry."

Castlecrag looks good. The streets are wide, the gardens are big, and the council picks up the rubbish. But at least on weekdays there doesn't seem to be a lot of life in the place. Maybe the kids are at boarding school and the wives are playing golf while the husbands take meetings. Maybe the wives are taking meetings, too. It's one of those suburbs where the groceries are delivered. Two-car, two-salary, two-dog territory.

The address Louise Madden had given me was a corner block in in one of the widest, quietest streets. There was a tennis court on the property and almost certainly a swimming pool behind the high brush fence. An archery range was a possibility.

I pushed a button at the set of wrought-iron gates mounted on brick pillars. I hoped I had the right address; it would be a fair hike to the front of the house next door. After a moderately long wait I saw Louise Madden begin the trek down the bricked driveway. She was wearing a denim smock and high-laced boots and carrying some kind of hooked implement which I never did identify. Her hair was tied up in a bright scarf, and the work gloves on her hands were yellow. She opened the gates, shucked off one glove, and shook my hand.

"Mr. Hardy," she said, "you look like you've been clearing privet."

I touched the scrapes and scratches last night's fun and games had left on my face. "Dealing with pests, certainly."

She waved me through the heavy gate and let it swing back. "We'll have to talk as I work. The woman here's a real bitch—wants it finished yesterday, and I'll get bawled out if I bend a blade of her precious grass."

"Fun to work for," I said. I had to hurry to

keep up with her as she strode down the path, which gave way to a series of gravel tracks that wound through the gardens. I was right about the swimming pool, and given the stands of tall native trees, I still considered the archery range an option.

"Some are; some aren't. She isn't. I take it you haven't found my dad?"

"No."

"And from the look of you, no good news."

"I don't think you can expect good news, Ms. Madden."

"He's dead?"

"Probably."

"Shit." She stopped and slashed at a bush with her hook. "How? Why?"

"I don't know yet. That's why I have to talk to you. Where are you working?"

"Over here." She led me across to a steep bank where she was setting railway sleepers into the earth. "Look good, don't they?"

"Yes."

She wiped a yellow glove across her face. Tears had cut through a thin film of dust, leaving pale streaks on her skin. She banged her hands together and sat down on a sleeper. "You'd better tell me about it."

"First, what d'you know about your grandfather?"

"Which one?"

"The who that built the bridge."

"Oh, Grandpa Madden. Yes." Through her distress over her father, memories of her grandfather caused her to smile. "He was great. But what's it got to do with—"

"Do the names Glover, Barclay, and"—I struggled to remember the names Meredith had mumbled and had to resort to my notebook—"Samuels and Booth mean anything to you?"

She shook her head. The sun went behind a cloud, and suddenly it was cold in the big garden. The light dropped, and the elegantly and strategically arranged plants looked grim and lifeless. Louise Madden unhooked a heavy cardigan from where it had been hanging on an embedded sleeper and shrugged into it. "Tell me what you're driving at."

"Several men, sons of engineers and others involved in the construction of the bridge, have vanished or died. There seems to be a connection."

She stood, picked up a mattock, and began hacking at the hard earth around a deeply implanted stump. "Got to move this if I'm going to get the layout right for Madam. I don't understand what you're saying."

"Neither do I."

"What were those names again?"

I gave them to her. She kept hacking, stopped, gave the stump a tug. It wobbled, just a little. "Dad knew a man named Samuels, I think. Yes. And he disappeared. That's right. I remember Dad talking about it."

"Was this Samuels somehow connected with the bridge?"

She put down the mattock and took off her cardigan. "I think he might have been. There was always a lot of talk about the bridge when we saw Grandpa. He was terribly proud of it."

"That's understandable," I said. "*I'm* proud of it, and all my dad ever did was drive over and help to pay for it."

"Mmm. Yes, now that you get me thinking about it, I believe Dad and Mr. Samuels did talk about the bridge. But they played golf together mostly. I don't think there was a Sons of the Bridge Builders Society or anything like that."

"No?" I watched her continue her attack on the stump. "I don't suppose your grandfather ever mentioned any enemies? Men with grudges against him?"

"Grandpa? He was just a sweet old man when I knew him. You'd think he'd have trouble climbing a ladder. But he told me he'd walked across the top of the arch after the bridge was finished, and I believed him. D'you think that could be true?"

I grinned. "Don't ask. Is there anything else you can tell me about your father, the bridge, friends connected with it? Anything like that?"

"No. Nothing. Did you find the woman? The woman Dad played golf with? You haven't asked me to—"

"I found her and talked to her. She couldn't help."

"What was she like?"

The mattock hung from her hand, forgotten. She was looking for something positive, some shred of comfort in a fatherless world. "Attractive and intelligent. She really cared for your father, and I think she misses him badly. But she—"

"Has a husband and property to protect. Kids." She swung the mattock viciously so that the blade stabbed three inches into the stump. "Fucking heteros!"

I was getting cold sitting there motionless in the shade. I stood and shivered. "I'm sorry to upset you, but these things don't usually work out too well."

"You warned me. You're doing your job. I understand. Give us a hand here."

I helped her to pull the mattock out of the stump, and the moment of friction passed. She gave off a nice smell—of earth and wood and leaves—and I wanted to touch her, to make contact with those good, healing things. She might have sensed this, might have misinterpreted. In any case she wasn't going to let it happen. She stepped back. "Do you need any more money, Mr. Hardy?"

"No."

She pointed to my head wounds. "You say they don't have anything to do with this case. Are you working on a couple of things at once? Not a good idea in my game." She waved a hand at the sleepers and mounds of earth.

"Nor in mine," I said. "The other thing's all

cleared up now. I can concentrate on finding out what happened to your father."

"Good," Louise Madden said.

I drove around for a while, looking for a place to buy a beer and a sandwich. On the way I passed a lot of houses that reminded me of the ones you see in Hollywood on the "homes of the rich and famous" tour. Here they were the homes of the rich and unknown, who preferred to stay that way. I ate the sandwich and drank the beer sitting in the car. From where I'd parked, I had a magnificent view of Middle Harbour. I speculated about why the rich always live in elevated positions and the less rich farther down the hill. My scratchy historical knowledge suggested it had been so since medieval times. That was an interesting thought. Was the position taken for reasons of safety, the last point to be attacked by an enemy, rather than domination? Were there exceptions in South America? It was the kind of half-baked question Helen and I used to have fun with. The people up here certainly looked safe. Or at least their houses did. There still weren't many actual people about. I flicked through my notebook again, underlining the names: Madden, Glover, Barclay, Samuels, Booth. Maybe some of them had lived in Castlecrag or similar places. Bellevue Hill was the same sort of location after all. But a lot of those high, medieval forts were stormed and taken, if memory served me right. Safety is an illusion.

I still wasn't fully recovered from my hectic night. I took a couple of aspirin with the last swallows of beer for my aching head, and the sun came out again and heated up the car, and I dozed off.

I woke up with that panicky feeling of not knowing where I was, or even who. Comprehension came back in a rush as I stared down at the water and the—from this distance— fragile-looking boats. Men were dead, men had vanished, and I was investigating how and why. Maybe other men were under threat, and here I was, sleeping in the afternoon. On the client's time. It occurred to me that the Glovers, Barclays, and others could probably afford the investigation better than Louise Madden. But they probably wouldn't want to pay me to sleep. The way things were going, billing Ms. Madden was going to be tricky. That led to thoughts of Cy Sackville and my court appearance. Maybe I should call him off and save some money. But Cy would be disappointed. Maybe we could sue the state for public mischief?

"And kiss your arse good-bye," I said aloud. I started the car and drove to Northbridge.

14

IT HAD BEEN SOME YEARS SINCE I'D BEEN TO PAUL AND PAT GUTHRIE'S HOUSE, BUT I found it without difficulty. The big peppercorn tree in front was unmistakable. Guthrie's block was wide and long with a deepwater frontage. Pretty flash, but after the place Louise Madden had been landscaping it looked modest. There were the usual couple of cars parked in the driveway, and the untidiness of the garden, giving the place a sort of weekender feel, was another thing I remembered and liked. A couple of dogs ran out and barked at me as I approached the house. Paul Guthrie wandered out onto the high deck that ran around three sides of the house to see what the dogs were barking at. When he saw me, he raised a hand in a vaguely naval salute and beckoned me forward.

I skirted the barbecue pit and the swimming pool, which had a heavy plastic cover over it. Guthrie came down a set of wooden steps from the deck. He must have been close to seventy, but he moved like a man twenty years younger. His handshake was firm without being competitive. When you've pulled oars for as long and as hard as he had, you don't need to show off your strength. Guthrie had been an Olympic sculler, and the strength and springiness needed for that tough event were still in him.

"Cliff," he said, "it's great to see you."

"Same here, Paul."

"What happened to your head?"

"The usual. How's life?"

Another man might have taken a quick look around his possessions before answering. Not Guthrie. "Pat's in the pink," he said. "The boys are fine. Two grandchildren, like I told you, and I can still row a boat. How would it be?"

"You're a lucky man, Paul."

"I know. Come inside and have a drink and tell me what you're up to."

We went into the house at ground level and down the wide passage to Guthrie's den, which housed his sporting trophies and family mementos—more of the latter than the former. He saw me settled in an armchair, went out whistling, and came back with two cans of light beer.

"Cheers," he said. "I suppose you got those

head wounds on that gambling boat the *Pava-rotti*?"

"Right. Ray was a big help there."

"Looks like you should've taken him along with you."

"Maybe. I hope he can help me some more." I touched the scratches. "But no rough stuff involved."

Guthrie nodded and waited. He was a discreet, experienced, levelheaded man, and there seemed no reason not to tell him about the Madden case. It sometimes helps to talk to an objective onlooker anyway. I gave it to him chapter and verse, and he listened in silence, sipping on his beer.

"Interesting," he said when I'd finished. "And you want to go and have a look in the water under the bridge?"

"Not me. Someone who knows how to handle himself in that situation. I thought Ray might know someone, be able to help with a boat, and so on."

"He will. And he'll do the dive himself. He's an expert, and he's always felt that he owes you a big favor."

I waved that away, or tried to. "I don't want him to feel like that. I just want to hire him to do a job. Perhaps you can help me to get it on that sort of footing, Paul."

"I'll try. When would you want to do this?"

"Tonight."

He broke into harsh, deep-chested laughter. "Jesus, Hardy, you're the limit. I should've known. Pat did. I said something about having you stay over for a night and go out on the harbor, and she said, 'He'll be off chasing someone.' "

I was saved from having to reply by the simultaneous arrival of Ray Guthrie and his mother. There was just enough light outside for me to see the little Honda and the Holden Jackaroo pulling up side by side in the driveway.

Pat Guthrie was a small dark woman with a trim figure and a worried look which gave way very attractively to merriment. She came across the grass and into the den, kissed her husband, and pointed a mock finger pistol at me. "Hullo, Cliff. You haven't changed much. A bit thinner, are you? Good to see you."

"You, too, Pat. You look well."

She nodded in Guthrie's direction. "We are. Has he shown you the snaps of the grandchildren yet?"

"Pat," Guthrie protested, "I'm not that doting, am I?"

"Just doting enough. Want another beer? Dinner'll be a while."

Guthrie patted his taut waistline and refused. I accepted. Pat smiled and left, and it was Ray Guthrie who brought in the can. I hadn't seen Ray since he and his girlfriend Jess Polansky had left Helen Broadway's flat in Elizabeth Bay. This was after I'd helped to send Ray's father to jail and shown him that his stepfather was the best friend he had in the world. Ray had broadened a bit, but the bulk looked to be due to hard work more than to self-indulgence. He was weather-beaten but not careworn. He looked happy. He shoved the beer at me, and we shook hands.

"How's Jess?" I said.

"Just great. Sends her best. She couldn't come, one of the kids is crook—"

"What?" Paul Guthrie almost jumped from his chair.

"Take it easy, Paul," Ray said. "It's nothing. She just needs her mum tonight."

"All right, but keep an eye on her."

Ray drank some beer and looked at his stepfather with affection. "You know, Cliff, he'd send to New York for the best fingernail man if one of them had something wrong with a fingernail."

Too much fond family feeling embarrasses me after a while. I hid the discomfort behind my can and an interest in the view from the window. The last of the daylight flickered out over the water. The lights on the moored boats in Middle Harbour and the glow in the sky across the water above Seaforth began to provide the sort of nightscape that justifies the mortgages. Paul Guthrie and his stepson were on such good terms that their casual talk was easy to drop in and out of. Pat came in and sat with a dry sherry for a while, and then she and Paul went off to put the finishing touches on the dinner.

"So," Ray said, "I told you how to get to the *Pavarotti* and you got bashed up?"

"Finished the job, though. It was useful information." I looked at Ray's solid jeans and windbreaker–covered figure. "I could've used you along at a couple of points, I admit."

"Try me now. What're you after?"

"Did Paul give you a hint?"

Ray shook his head. "Mr. Discretion, Paul. I've come to realize that a good stepfather is better than a real father in a way. He can move aside, let you grow up. Both Chris and me have benefited."

I nodded. Chris was Ray's brother, who'd also struck trouble a few years back. Now he was a graduate in something or other and employed in New Guinea. Their father, who knew too many things, had been killed in what had been called an accident in the industrial section of Long Bay prison.

"Done any scuba diving, Ray?"

"Plenty. Love it."

"What's the depth of the water under the harbor bridge?"

Ray fiddled with his empty can, crushing its sides. Unlike his brother, he was a practical man who liked to have something to see and handle in front of him. Theoretical questions, or those requiring information to be transferred from one track to another, made him uncomfortable. "I've got a Maritime Services Board chart on the boat that'd tell me," he said. "At a guess, twenty meters. Certainly not more. That's average—high and low tide."

"Is that a deep dive?"

"Are you kidding? Piece of piss. Course, it'd be murky down there. Lot of crap in the harbor."

"What about at night?"

He leaned forward in his chair. "*Very* murky. But you can take down a light that makes it okay."

"What about a camera?"

"Christ, Cliff." He leaned back and crushed the can vertically. When he'd reduced it to the size of a doughnut, he looked at me and grinned. "Why not?"

"This isn't *Mission Impossible*, Ray. If it's too bloody hard to handle, I'll come at it another way."

"I can dive around the bridge at night and take photos," Ray said. "When d'you want it done?"

"Tonight," I said.

That's when Paul Guthrie called us in to dinner.

Fish, naturally, in that company. All I know about fish is that when it's fresh and well cooked, I like it, and when it's not, I don't. This was great. The Guthries treated one another as a group of special friends might: quick to understand and sympathize, happy to chide and be chided. But I didn't feel excluded. I enjoyed the talk and the meal and the dry white. Ray, I noticed, drank mineral water and talked less than the rest of us. Ate less, too.

Almost as soon as he decently could, he wiped his mouth on the paper towel provided, collected his couple of plates, and stood. "Excuse me. Great dinner . . ."

"You hardly touched it," Pat Guthrie said. "Are you sure you're not sick, too?"

"I'm fine. I just have to make a few phone calls." His nod was more for me than his parents as he left the room.

"Sorry," I said, "I've asked Ray for some help. He seems to have taken it very seriously."

"It's all right, Cliff," Paul said. "Ray's like that. He takes things seriously. I remember once when he—"

"Don't start, Paul," his wife said. "And don't keep things from me. What are you asking Ray to do, Cliff?"

I told her as we cleared up the dishes and took them to the kitchen, where she stacked them in the washer. "Aren't there regulations about that?" she said. "I mean, can anyone just go diving around the bridge? I wouldn't have thought so."

"Ray'll know," Paul Guthrie said from the doorway. "Or he'll know someone who will know. Don't worry."

Pat turned on the machine. "It sounds dangerous. At night. No preparation. Why does it have to be like that?"

Paul Guthrie was spooning coffee into a glass beaker. He poured in the boiling water and set the plunger in place. "*Is* it dangerous, Cliff?"

"Ray doesn't seem to think so. But I'll call it off if it gets tricky. Don't worry, I'm too old for cowboy stuff."

"So we've noticed," Paul said. He touched his own forehead, which wasn't scratched and scraped like mine.

I grinned. "I was assisting the police. Pat, it has to be at night to avoid publicity. The woman I'm working for has a right to that. Anything to do with mysterious deaths brings headlines. Team that up with the bridge and you've got a tabloid reporter's dream."

Guthrie pressed the plunger down. He set the pot, cups, sugar, and milk on a tray. "Let's go through to the sitting room. I saw them building the bridge, you know. Went to the opening ceremony and everything."

We got settled with the coffee. Paul took some artificial sweeteners from a shelf and dropped in two tablets. "I'm seventy this year," he said. "Milk, Cliff?"

Pat laughed as she took a half spoon of sugar. "He'll take it black, Paul. He's a tough guy." For a moment I thought that Pat Guthrie might be turning against me, protecting her young from the sort of disruption I represented. But she included me in the amusement. "And don't you come the smart-arse old-timer. Tell us about the bridge."

"They say a million people went across it on

the first day," I said. "I never really believed that."

"I do," Paul said. "I can't tell you much about the ceremony. I was there, but way back in the crowd. I know I've never seen so many people in one place before. I didn't see de Groot. There was just a series of yells and shouts and screams. I think I fell asleep that afternoon somewhere along the line."

"I'm more interested in the industrial aspects," I said.

Guthrie's thumb and third finger probed the grooves in his cheeks. "My father was captain of one of the tugboats that helped to build the bridge."

"What did the tugboats do?" Pat asked.

"A lot of the superstructure was built onshore and taken out to where it was needed on barges. The it was hoisted up into place. The tugs pulled the barges."

"I've seen some photographs of that operation," I said. "Must've been pretty tricky in bad weather."

Guthrie nodded. "It was. The whole bloody thing was tricky. It's a wonder more people weren't killed."

Pat was about to sip her coffee, but she stopped the movement. "I didn't know people were killed."

"Quite a few," Guthrie said. "In the quarry at Moruya, in the workshop, on the bridge. I saw all of it. I was only a nipper, but my dad was interested, and he took me around. He could go anywhere he liked, of course."

Paul had forgotten his half-drunk coffee. He was settled back in his chair with his memories. Knowing the sharpness of his mind and the clarity of his perceptions, I believed the memories would be distinct. "What were the working conditions like?" I said.

"By today's standards, terrible, and pretty bad even by the standards of the 1920s and 1930s. You have to remember that it was bloody hard to get work then. Men'd do amazing things for a couple of quid a week when they had mouths to feed."

"I've never thought about it," Pat said. "The bridge has always been sort of . . . there."

"Well, it wasn't. It was the most amazing thing to see those two bloody great arches grow out on either side and finally join up. It seemed, I don't know, like something almost impossible for men to achieve. It made a very deep impression on me, even though I was so young. My dad was a bit of a bolshie, and he used to talk about the cost of the thing in human terms."

"Deaths and injuries," I said.

"Yes. There was nothing in the papers about the injuries, except the occasional bit of bullshit from the managers."

"Like what?" I asked.

Guthrie made a derisive, snorting sound. "Oh, about how the workers were like soldiers going into battle, and casualties were inevitable. That sort of thing. My dad used to read stuff like that out from the papers. It made him angry. I saw things that make me angry to think about them even now."

"What, Paul?" Pat had put her cup down and was staring at her husband.

Guthrie rubbed his hand across his face. He looked around his comfortable, well-appointed sitting room as if he could hardly believe in the reality of his surroundings. "One thing in particular. I can see it now, and I still don't like to think about it. Dad had taken me to the fabrication workshop. It was where Luna Park is now. They built big sections and took them out on the barges. They used a hot-rivet method."

Pat shook her head. "You've lost me."

Guthrie's eyes seemed to retreat into his skull. "They heated the rivets up, almost to liquid point. Then they spooned them across to the riveter, who had heavy gloves and tongs. He lifted the bit of red-hot metal out and banged it into place. It was incredibly dangerous."

"This is in the workshop," Pat said, "not—"

"They did the same up on the structure. Tossed this red-hot metal around as if it was putty."

"It sounds sort of . . . Dickensian," Pat said.

Guthrie struggled up out of his recollection. "How do you mean, love?"

"Well, like workhouses, sweated labor, children down the mines . . . that sort of thing."

Guthrie shook his head. "No. It was nothing like that. Not as I recall it. The reverse, if anything. The men were happy, cheerful, laughing. Anyway, this time I remember, a rivet jumped out of the dish or slipped from the tongs. I don't know. It happened so quick. The rivet hit him somewhere around here." Guthrie touched his thigh. "And it burned through his overalls and went down inside them. He was screaming and screaming. . . . Dad grabbed me and pulled me away."

Ray Guthrie's head appeared around the door. "We're on," he said.

15

THREE HOURS LATER I WAS SITTING IN A BOAT UNDER THE SYDNEY HARBOUR BRIDGE. Not exactly under, a bit to the side and near the north shore, but close enough. Aboard were Ray Guthrie and another man whom he'd introduced as Milo. Like Ray and me, Milo was wearing a parka and a woolen knit cap and trying to expose as little of himself to the cold air as possible. It had been very cold on the run from Northbridge to this point. Here, somewhat sheltered from the wind, it wasn't so bad. But the people in the restaurants—the Imperial Palace, picked out in lights, and Doyles at the Quay, spelled out in blue neon—were showing a lot more sense than we were.

I was mindful of Pat Guthrie when I asked Ray how dangerous the operation was likely to be.

"How d'you mean?"

"Oh well, sharks, getting tangled up in something under the water, electric cables . . ."

Ray laughed. "Hear that, Milo? Electric cables. Listen, Cliff, we've got only two problems."

I could hear Milo chuckling as he did something with ropes. "They are?"

"One, the water police come along and ask us what we're doing. That's your department."

"Two?"

"Some amateur could come along and hit us. That's Milo's department."

"Ready, Ray?" Milo said.

"Yeah." Ray went into the little cabin of the boat and came back a few minutes later in wet suit and flippers. Milo helped him strap on a tank while they adjusted his goggles and talked about pressure and currents.

I stared around me, feeling extraneous. I could hear a pontoon mooring creaking over on the quay side, and there was a red light blinking on the near shore. I couldn't identify the light. The city loomed up on both sides, towers of partly lit steel and glass. The surface of the water was dark but fairly calm. At least I wasn't asking him to go down in the middle of a howling gale. I still didn't feel good about it, though. What would I say to Paul and Pat if . . .

"Cliff," Milo said, "we got no problem about the light." He gestured to a tube Ray had tucked in his belt and a camera enclosed in a rubber case and fastened to his arm with a heavy elastic strap. "That's an Ikelite modular job—the best. Hard to say what the visibility'll be like. Could be a couple of meters; could be more. Depends on the particles in the water. If it's bad, the light won't help much. Be like headlights coming at you through a dirty windshield. But we could be lucky. Pictures might be a bit of a problem."

"Do the best you can, Ray," I said. "You might not see anything anyway." I'd explained to Ray that I wanted him to explore the area immediately under the bridge for as much of the fourteen-hundred-foot stretch as possible, but concentrating on the middle. I told him what he was looking for; it didn't seem to worry him. I didn't ask him how he'd know where he was once he was under the water. Apparently it wasn't a problem. Ray dipped his mask in a bucket of water and flapped it around. Then he pulled it over his face and took two froggy steps to the side of the boat. I thought he'd do a backflip, like the ones Lloyd Bridges used to do in *Sea Hunt*, but he just climbed over and slipped down into the dark, lapping water.

A bit of threshing on the surface, and he was gone. Milo started the engine, and the boat puttered across to the Milson's Point shore. "Can't stick around out there like a shag on a rock."

"Won't he need a marker or something? How's he to know where he is?"

"He'll come up to five meters or so and look up at the bridge lights. Vertical visibility under water's better than horizontal. He'll be right. Fifteen meters, twenty at the most. Piece of piss. Don't look so worried, Cliff. Ray's a top scuba man. Top."

"What about you, Milo?"

"I'm pretty bloody good, too."

"You'd better be," I said, "because there's no way I'm going down there if he gets the cramp."

Milo laughed. "If he gets cramp, he comes up. It's only fifteen bloody meters. He's not going to get the bends."

I grunted. "People drown in the bath."

"Jesus, you're a happy one. Australians're supposed to be cheerful bastards."

"No," I said, "that's Greeks."

He laughed again. I was the funniest act on the harbor that night. It was too late for the ferries, and there was nothing else moving on the water. I could hear the intermittent rumble of traffic on the bridge above and an occasional crash from the container wharf at Mort Bay. Milo lit a cigarette and hummed as he made adjustments to the line hanging into the water. He checked his watch and started the engine.

I was too nervous to have any idea of the time. "How long's he been down?"

Milo held up his thumb and forefinger an

inch apart. "About this much of his tank. Don't worry about him. We just gotta watch for trouble up here."

The red light fascinated me. I located it in Kirribilli, where the prime minister and the governor-general sometimes live. I wondered if they were there tonight, perhaps together, toasting the revolution. Probably not, on all scores.

"Need any help there?"

The voice, amplified through cupped hands, came from a man sitting in a dinghy a few feet away from our boat. He'd shipped one of his oars and was using the other to keep the dinghy more or less stationary. On closer inspection the boat was something more than a dinghy. It was wider and flatter-looking and had provision for a sail and a couple of large lockers built into the structure. Milo shone a torch on him, and he lifted a dark-gloved hand to block out the beam. He was wearing a tracksuit and sneakers and a long-peaked cap that kept his face shadowed. He wasn't young.

"We're fine," I said. "How about you?"

"Just rowing about. Habit of mine. Don't see too many people around here at night. Would you think me too rude if I asked what you're doing? Free to refuse to answer, of course."

His voice was that of a man habituated to politeness, but it didn't cut any ice with Milo. I hadn't thought nerves were part of his makeup, but he showed I was wrong. "We're minding our own business, mate," he growled. "Why don't you do the same?"

The rower slipped his oar into the rowlock and pulled away expertly without responding.

"Bit rude, Milo," I said. "What's the matter?"

"Bloody nutter. I dunno. This place gives me the creeps."

It was getting to me, too; I realized for the first time that the bridge was blocking the light from a low-lying half-moon, leaving us in a deep, inky shadow. "Where do you reckon Ray is now?" I said.

Milo shrugged. "What would you have told that old joker?"

"I was just starting to think. Probably would have told him I was a private detective hired to find something that'd been dropped overboard from a Balmain ferry."

"Fuck me," Milo said. "What a bullshit artist."

We were saved from falling out even further by a noise in the water. Ray surfaced about seventy-five feet away and swam toward us. Milo started the engine. I helped Ray climb aboard, and we were moving away as soon as he was properly over the side. He gave Milo a nod, slipped the light from his belt, and unhooked the camera. I was unfamiliar with the apparatus, and clumsy, but I helped him to shuck off the tank. When he pulled off the mask, his face was unnaturally white, and his lips were drawn back in a tight, jaw-locked grin.

"You okay?" I said.

He gulped and nodded. "There's some brandy down in the cabin. I could do with a belt."

I went down and got the bottle of Tolley's brandy. I uncapped it, and Ray took a big swig. I did the same and held it out toward Milo. He shook his head.

"Not while he's driving," Ray said.

We were skipping across the water, passing Kirribilli, where the red light was still blinking. Ray had another drink.

"Well?" I said.

Ray toweled himself off and wrapped a blanket around his shoulders. "Three of them. Could be more. But three was enough for me. Short chains to plugs of some kind. They're all wrapped in canvas. I touched one. Squishy. Pretty close together. More or less in the dead set middle under the bridge. Jesus, Cliff, you should've seen them. In the light. Sort of . . . half floating, half hanging there."

I started to say something about being sorry to put him through it, but he didn't listen. He looked out at the water and the land and drew in several deep breaths, as if trying to cleanse his insides. Then he shivered and went below to get changed. Milo had another cigarette going, and I was tempted to ask him for one. I resisted. I hadn't earned the right to the weakness. I wasn't the one who'd seen the canvas shrouds. That led me to think of the camera. I picked it up and then heard Milo clicking his fingers. I handed the camera to him.

"You get what you wanted?" he said.

"Worse than I expected, apparently."

"Must be, to shake Ray up. He's a tough bastard."

"I know. That's why I . . ."

He held the wheel with one hand and examined the camera. When he was satisfied, he set it down at his feet. "He got a few shots for you. Could be they'll come out okay."

"I want to thank you for your help," I said. "I felt pretty edgy out there."

"That's all right. Sorry I got shitty. I felt as if the fuckin' bridge was going to fall down on us."

We were well out in the channel, in choppy water, making for Bradleys Head. I passed the brandy bottle to Milo. "Have a drink," I said. "I'm sure you know your way back from here."

16

THE BRANDY BOTTLE TRAVELED BACK AND FORTH A FEW TIMES ON THE PASSAGE to Middle Harbour. Ray changed his clothes and had one of Milo's cigarettes. He was pretty shaken, and I was sorry I'd put him through it.

"What was Paul talking about just before I came in?" he asked.

"He was telling your mother and me how things were when they built the bridge."

"How were they?"

"Bloody hard and dangerous."

Ray rubbed a towel over his head, but oil and grease from the harbor water remained. He looked at the towel. "Harbor's filthy. Weird, isn't it? The water was probably very clean back then, but they treated workers like shit. Now the workers get a fair go, and the environment's a great big toilet."

I agreed that it was weird.

"What happened to those blokes? I suppose they *were* blokes?"

The question hadn't occurred to me: Were the daughters of the bridge builders also under threat? I was too tired and stressed to give Ray a full answer. I just told him that the bodies were those of missing people and that there was some connection with the bridge. "I can count on you to keep quiet about this, Ray, can't I?"

"Absolutely. Milo, too. And don't insult me by offering me money."

"What about Milo?"

"He won't be insulted."

I gave Milo fifty bucks and thanked him for his help. "Sure," Milo said. "What's next? Do we climb Centrepoint?"

"Don't laugh, Cliff," Ray said. "He could do it."

We stowed the gear, and Ray shut and locked the hatches and doors on the boat. Milo said good night, jumped up onto the dock, and walked off. I heard a car engine start and tires gripping gravel. Ray said he'd have a shower in his parents' house and go home. "Paul'll wake up no matter how quiet I am," he said. "Want to see him?"

I considered. "I wouldn't want to disturb him."

Ray stepped onto the dock and juggled the camera as he helped me up. "No problem. He sleeps so light you wouldn't believe it. He'd be happy to say good night, or good morning, or whatever the hell it is."

We walked through the semitropical garden the Guthries had growing between their house and the water. It wasn't nearly as cold here as out on the harbor, and I pulled off the woolen cap and the parka. Ray was still rubbing grease from his head when we went into the house. He went away to shower, and I hung the parka on a peg by the back door. Almost as soon as the water started to run, Paul Guthrie appeared in the hallway.

"What's the time?" he said.

"I don't know. About four."

"Find what you were looking for?"

I nodded.

"You want some tea?"

"I never drink tea, Paul. I'll have some coffee if you're making. How come you wake up so easily?"

He grinned. With his crew-cut hair sticking up and his trim body wrapped in a smart Asian-print dressing gown he looked like a fit fifty-year-old. "Used to be from worry, when I agonized about business twenty-four hours a day. Now, I don't know. I think I just like it. I get up for an hour or so most nights. It's quiet, and you can think clearly."

We went through to the kitchen, and he put water on to boil. We sat on stools and waited. "How did it go tonight?"

"Good. Ray comes through, doesn't he?"

"Always. He's sound. Pat's always worried

that he and Chris're going to show signs of going to the bad, like their father. I tell her it won't happen, and I reckon I'm right." The water boiled, and Paul made tea for himself and instant coffee for me. The shower was still running.

"Ray came up looking like a Channel swimmer," I said. "Grease in the water."

Paul shook his head. "It's a crying shame. You wouldn't believe how dirty the harbor and the coast have got. Well, you have to believe it, after all the publicity. But I've seen it happening over the years. Couldn't get anyone to listen—councillors, politicians. Hopeless bloody bunch."

I sipped the hot, milky coffee and felt it blend warmly and comfortingly with the brandy in my stomach. My mind was tired but still working sluggishly on the case. "I don't suppose your father's still alive, Paul? I need to—"

Guthrie snapped his fingers and jumped off the stool. "That's what I have to do. That's why I got up. Hang on."

I drank some coffee. The shower stopped running. Guthrie came back carrying a thick book. "You missed Dad by only a few years," he said. "Lived into his nineties. After you left, I got to thinking about the bridge and all that. I hunted around and found this." He held out the book. "It's Dad's scrapbook on the bridge. He kept it for years, from the time he captained the tug and until after the opening. Thought it might be useful."

The scrapbook was an old-fashioned seaman's log with clippings and papers pasted to the leaves. It was only about an inch wide at the spine but four inches wide at the edges of the leaves. Some of the clippings had been too big for the page and were folded over; others had frayed and torn edges. I turned over a few pages and saw newspaper reports on the men and the work. "It could be very useful, Paul. Can I take it away? I'm too bushed to—"

"Of course, of course. Take it. Give it back when you've finished your inquiry. That'll force you to come and see us again. Here, I'll get you something to put it in."

He rummaged in the cupboard for a plastic bag and found one just as Ray walked into the kitchen. "Shouldn't use those things, Paul," he said. "You should see them in the harbor. It's chocka."

Guthrie straightened up and handed me the bag. "I know. I know." He glanced at Ray. "You okay, son?"

Ray nodded and unscrewed the lid of the coffee jar. "Reckon I can get the pictures developed later tomorrow. I mean, today. You know."

I put the scrapbook in the plastic bag and tied its handles together. "Thanks. I'll give you a ring."

Paul Guthrie said, "You've found your client's father then, Cliff?"

"Odds-on."

"Poor woman, but it's better to know than to wonder." He was speaking from experience, as a man who'd had a time of wondering whether his stepson was alive or dead.

I shook hands with both of them and left, carrying the scrapbook encased in polluting plastic. It sat beside me on the passenger seat as I drove home. *Live to ninety and leave behind scrapbooks on your big jobs. And the love and respect of a son,* I thought. *Not bad, Captain Guthrie, sir. Not bad at all.*

I woke up late and eased into the day gently. A long, hot shower got rid temporarily of the ache in my kicked ribs and helped with the stiffness that had come from positioning a forty-plus-year-old body on a boat on Sydney Harbor on a cold winter night. My cuts and bruises were healing well, though; maybe it was the sea air. For want of better company, I'd taken the scrapbook to bed with me. I hauled it out to read while I drank several cups of coffee. I threw the plastic bag in the rubbish bin, wondering vaguely where it would end up.

Inside the cover Paul's father had written: "David Alexander Guthrie, MM, tug *Hercules,* 1926–32." What followed was a personal history of the building of the bridge. Captain Guthrie had taken photographs of his tug at work and the various stages of bridge construction. There were also pictures of the quarry at Moruya and the fabrication work-shop Paul had spoken about. These were glued into the book and captioned. Letters from the captain's employer were similarly attached. They replied to complaints about the safety of the barge moorings and the suitability of the tackle used to lift the materials aloft. Faded blue-carbon copies of Guthrie's letters testified to his continued concern. To judge from the replies, he got little satisfaction. There were death notices for some of the workers killed, and a clipping from the *Labor Daily*, which Guthrie had annotated "Lang paper" for February 10, 1932:

James Campbell had been engaged in dis-mantling the scaffolding near the top of the pylon. A strong gust of wind moved the beam on which he was standing, and he was hurled into space. Horrified watchers in the streets below saw him shoot out from the pylon, turning over and over as he clutched wildly for something to stay his flight. . . . He fell to the ground through the open structure near the footway.

It wasn't all gloom and doom. Guthrie had recorded the great moments, such as the clos-ing of the arch and the hanging of the last section of the deck. There were newspaper photographs of the opening ceremony and a couple of the captain's own creditable efforts. One shot, captioned "Self & Hercules," showed a stocky man with a pipe jutting from his jaw standing at a ship's wheel. Not enough of his face was visible under the cap and beard to mark a resemblance to Paul Guthrie, but the stubborn, almost aggressive stance was unmistakable.

Fascinated by the material and almost forgetting why I was in possession of it, I leafed through the book. A photograph of sober-looking men in high collars and dark suits brought me back to the present. Here they were, the builders: Barclay, Glover, Bradfield, Ennis, Samuels, Madden, Booth, Bondil—more than a dozen of them, with each man's function neatly assigned to him. Most of the faces were mustached or bearded. Bradfield, generally considered the father of the bridge, was among the clean-shaven brigade. I checked off the names against the areas of operation. Joseph Samuels was the proprietor and manager of the foundry attached to the fabrication workshop. Reginald Booth was the director of public works.

Captain Guthrie had circled in red a clipping that contained a statement from Lawrence Ennis, a chief of one of the major engineering firms involved in the job. It might not have been the statement Paul Guthrie remembered, but it was pretty close: "Every day those men went onto the bridge they went in the same way as a soldier goes into battle, not knowing whether they would come down alive or not."

I poured my third cup and settled down to accumulate my notes and materials on the Madden case. I had the scrapbook, photocopies, my own notes. By the end of the day I hoped to have some photographs. Maybe I'd found Brian Madden, maybe not. Determining where my responsibility began and ended was a tricky matter. If I reported everything to the police, and they arranged to raise the canvas-wrapped bodies from the harbor, the story, in all its ghoulish detail, would get out. All the names involved would be published, and the careers of the bridge builders and their families exposed to scrutiny. Somehow I didn't think Louise Madden would like that. And there was no guarantee that her father was one of the victims.

So much for the private uncertainties. There was also the public, community consideration. Descendants of the bridge builders weren't wrapping themselves in canvas, tying something heavy to their legs, and throwing themselves into the harbor. Someone was killing them. That someone had fouled up with Colin Glover, the floater. Maybe he was getting careless. If so, now was the best time to try to catch him. And there was nothing surer than that a welter of publicity and tabloid headlines like BRIDGE KILLER DUBBED "DAVY JONES" BY POLICE would cause him to stop or become super-careful.

I was puzzling over these questions when the telephone rang. I looked at the instrument with dislike; it was unlikely to have any answers. But I picked it up.

"Hardy."

"Mr. Hardy? My name's Ralph Wren. I believe Frank Parker told you I'd be calling."

"You're right, he did. How's Meredith?"

"Ah . . . I'm not quite sure."

Ah, a careerist, I thought, *more concerned to get on than about his colleague. Frank's losing the ability to pick them.* I decided there and then how I was going to proceed. "I spoke to him yesterday, Mr. Wren," I said. "He seemed to be doing pretty well."

"Good, good," Wren said. "About this case . . ."

"Have you got Meredith's paperwork?"

"He . . . ah, doesn't go in for a lot of paperwork. I was hoping you could help me out there."

I was confirmed in my decision. "I don't know . . . Constable, is it?"

"Detective sergeant."

"Detective Sergeant Wren, right. I don't think I can help you. What did Frank Parker tell you?"

Wren's tone became waspish. "He said you'd be cooperative."

"I am. I want to be. What do you want to know?"

"Mr. Hardy, this isn't helpful. Meredith was pursuing a line of inquiry that crossed with something you were doing. That's all I know."

"Well, I haven't done anything more, Sergeant. I'm pretty much in the dark until I can have a proper talk with Meredith. I think that's a good way off, don't you?"

"I don't know."

"Tell you what. You keep an eye on Meredith, and we'll have a three-way meeting when he's fit. I think that's a good idea, don't you?"

"Possibly, I—"

"Let's leave it there. I'll call Frank and tell him we've spoken. Probably have to leave a message for him; he wasn't exactly chatty when I saw him. You can get in touch with me again when you think Meredith's up to it. Give him my regards on your next visit, okay?"

I hung up gently and let my hand hover over the phone. If he didn't call straight back, it probably meant I'd bluffed him sufficiently to gain the time I needed. If he did call, I had the option of not answering. The phone didn't ring. I shuffled through the documents again, made out a list of names, and laid the lot out like cards on a table. But my hand came out the same way: My only lead was the the Veterans of the Bridge and the address in Pump Street. I collected together the few things I thought I'd need: burglary tools, miniature tape recorder, key card. I said aloud, "When you can't carry a gun, carry cash." I sniggered and then realized what I was doing. I'd been living alone too long.

The phone rang as I was heading for the door. I considered not answering it, but phones are about the only things that incline me to believe in the paranormal; often I can *feel* who's calling. Sometimes I'm right. This time I *felt* it wasn't Ralph Wren. Right again. It was Cy Sackville.

"Well, Cliff," Cy said, coming the breezy barrister, "I've poked around a bit and they don't—"

"It's off, Cy."

"What do you mean it's off? This is a serious matter. It's your livelihood to start with, and it could be your liberty."

"You've been rehearsing," I said.

"A little. I'm looking forward to it. The precedents are most interesting."

"No doubt. I'm sorry, but I have to disappoint you. The matter got cleared up the other night. There was a conspiracy against me. I was an innocent victim."

One of Cy's strengths is his quick recovery. He'd have shrugged and moved something else up on his agenda, even though this little legal byway had interested him more than some he'd gone down with me. "I'm delighted to hear it," he said. "In fact, that was the sort of line I was going to pursue."

"Thanks, Cy, but it's not going to go any further. One of the conspirators is dead, and one of the others is in custody. They've got him for conspiracy to murder and malicious wounding, for starters."

"I see."

"Sorry to waste your time."

"No matter. I learned some things about a

piece of legislation. It'll come in useful some time. And of course, I'll bill you for the work."

"Of course."

We both knew he wouldn't. He'd get payment in kind from me by having me do some work for him, or he'd simply forget. Cy is an old-time, wishy-washy socialist and guilty about the amount of money he makes. So would I be if I made a quarter as much.

"Are you okay, Cliff? Are you really in the clear, or is there something I can do?"

"I'm in the clear on that matter. Listen, Cy, if someone found some bodies and didn't report them, what would the charges be?"

"Concealing evidence."

"Obstructing the police?"

"Yes."

"Committing public nuisance?"

"Possibly."

"Imperiling inquiry agent license?"

"I wouldn't be surprised."

"Neither would I. Thanks, Cy." I shivered as I spoke. The biggish house was cold; drafts came in under the doors, and a decayed window frame was rattling upstairs, troubled by a strong, cold south wind.

"What's wrong?"

"Nothing. Know a good solicitor around here?"

"Paul Hart in Balmain. Why? Look, Cliff, d'you mean your will? If you're in trouble, tell me. I can—"

"I'm thinking about selling this bloody house, Cy. That's all. Thanks. See you."

If you can't carry a gun, carry cash. Very neat. Well, I couldn't carry a gun because the police had taken mine after the fracas in the Kings Cross alley, and I hadn't been interested enough at the time to ask for it back. I used to have an unlicensed Colt .45 which I kept for emergencies in a clip under the dashboard of my old Falcon. But the old Falcon let in water, and the firing pin on the Colt had rusted solid. *What the hell?* I thought. *No veteran of the bridge is going to be under seventy. Carry cash.* I deposited Louise Madden's check, drew out a couple of hundred, and drove to the Rocks.

17

MY REASONING WAS THIS: SOMEONE CONNECTED WITH THE VETERANS OF THE BRIDGE
Society was killing the descendants of the
bridge builders. Motive uncertain. Revenge?
Retribution? Insanity almost certainly part of
the picture. Probably, therefore, the perpetra-
tor was connected with someone who'd been
killed while working on the bridge. That gave
me the list of names. The list was dauntingly
Anglo-Saxon and ordinary: McKeon, Addison,
Campbell, and the like. There would be thou-
sands of people by those names now living in
the city. But it was a starting point. As I drove,
I recalled a section in Spearritt's book headed
"Driven to Death." According to Spearritt,
more than 150 people had died by jumping
from the bridge. If they were factored in, as
the experts on the radio say, the net would be

cast even wider. How many people connected with the 150 jumpers would there be? It sounded like a job for Professor Spearritt and his computer. What about people killed in car crashes on the bridge? What about the people whose TV reception was buggered up by all the metal? The more I thought that way, the more I was reminded that there were more than five million rivets in the bridge. It would be hell of a job looking for just one of them.

Pump Street was quiet and oddly dusty. The dust must have drifted from construction sites nearby and settled there, because there was no actual building work going on in the street itself. It gave the landscape an old-world historical flavor, as if nothing much had changed since the streets were unpaved and there was more horse dung on the road than oil stains. I drove slowly along the street, turned at the end, and looked for the laneway that usually runs behind rows of Sydney terraces. No laneway, or rather, there had been a lane, but the redbrick building I had noticed before, which I now identified as a bond store, had annexed it sometime in the past, and there was now no back entrance to the houses. Not good. I didn't want to be held up again by Betty Tracey or provide entertainment for the diversion-starved residents of Pump Street.

I parked opposite number 47, a few doors along from 43A, and saw the solution to my problem. At the end of the terrace, just before a series of semidetached houses began, there was a narrow gap. I crossed the street and inspected the opening to a passage scarcely wide enough to squeeze through and not passable by anyone really bulky. All Alan Bond's millions wouldn't get him down there. I negotiated it, although I felt I had to hold my breath and suck in my stomach. Also, I had to twist myself sideways to make the turn where the passage went right, parallel to the street and behind the houses. The opposing wall was high and brick, part of the lane-annexing bond store. The backyards to the houses were almost nonexistent—tiny bricked or cemented squares with brick outhouse toilets, not even enough space for a Hills Hoist. There were wooden fences, much patched with galvanized iron and other materials and gates from the lane, opening in toward the houses. With the gate open, a rubbish bin in place, and a six-pack, the yard would be full to capacity.

Some of the gates had listed so badly they were immovable; the hinges on others had rusted solid; a few had been nailed or boarded shut or simply built over. By squinting up at the backs of the houses and trying to calculate where the divisions of the terrace fell, I reckoned I was able to distinguish the back of number 43A. The house differed in no way from the others—same rusty iron roof, drooping guttering, and water-stained walls—but the gate was firm on its posts, and the hinges had been recently oiled. The paving in the lane was a sort of cobblestone that had cracked and lifted in places, further impeding the opening of the gates. But at the gate of 43A the paving had been mended, pounded flat. My theory—that someone had been listening in the house when I'd made my inquiry about Stan Livermore and had had the time and means to leave and kill old Stan—was looking stronger. *Look for a lean man,* I thought, *with an oilcan and a mallet.*

I braced my back against the brick wall and inched my feet up the solid gatepost until I was high enough to straddle the gate and climb over. The gate had a simple barrel bolt, which I slid back experimentally—smooth as silk. I left it open and approached the house. A short light access on the right-hand side, a narrow set of brick steps to the back door, and a decayed, unfastened flywire screen with too many holes in it to keep flies out, let alone trouble burglars. On the solid door was a mortised lock, old and loose. A jiggle with a piece of thin metal (plastic never works for me), a downward pressure and twist on the handle, and I had the door open. Not exactly a break and enter, more a bend and enter.

I was in a small back porch which had been boarded up and provided with a couple of small windows. There was a narrow bed and about a seventhhand cupboard; a cardboard box by the bed contained dirty socks and several copies of a racing tip sheet. Somehow this didn't look like the room of the late Stan Livermore, secretary of the Veterans of the

Bridge Society. I went through a curtained doorway to the kitchen, which was like old kitchens everywhere in the city: lino on the surfaces, brass on the plumbing, and cockroaches in the woodwork. There was a smell of some sort in the air, vaguely sweet and recognizable. The stove was still hot, and I found an empty Rosella tomato soup can in a bucket under the sink. Memories of a Sydney boyhood. We used to pour a bit into the mugs, top up the can with milk, and heat it. No saucepans, no spoons. Somewhere in this house was a traditionalist.

I moved through to the passage which led to the stairs. I know these kinds of houses. On ground level there'd be a front room, with the window opening onto the street, and two rooms upstairs. A bathroom off the landing. The veranda to the front room up top would be built in, like the porch below. During the Depression these houses slept up to twenty people. My guess was that Betty Tracey occupied the front room by the door. That'd give her the greatest control over the movements of the people in the house. First grab at visitors and the mail, best snoop at the street. I went quietly down to the door and listened but there was no sound. No chance of Betty's being the soup eater. I was pretty sure you'd be able to hear her at it from the backyard.

That left the stairs, which from the look of them—rickety treads, gap-toothed banisters, lifting lino—would certainly creak. No chance of surprise. I marched up the first flight calling, "Mr. Livermore. Mr. Livermore! Are you in?"

A man appeared at the top of the stairs. "Who are you?" he said. "How did you get in here?"

"Mrs. Tracey let me in. I met her outside." I waved my hand in the direction of the street. "I paid her five dollars, and she let me in."

"Five dollars, mmm. That'll keep her happy in the pub for a few hours." He came down the stairs far enough into the dim light to enable me to see him. Bald, sixty maybe, strong-looking, in a heavy cable-knit sweater and flannel trousers. "Didn't she tell you Mr. Livermore was dead?"

"No. No, she didn't. I'm sorry to hear that. Recently, was it?"

"The other day. She's a shameless old extortionist. That's what she is. Well, afraid that's the way of it."

"Ah, I'm a journalist. Brian Kelly. I was hoping to talk to Mr. Livermore about the Veterans of the Bridge Society. Thought there might be a piece in it, you know. Mr.?"

"Lithgow, Charles Lithgow. A journalist, eh? I'm a bit of a writer myself. Who d'you write for, Mr. Kelly?"

"Free-lance." I went up a few more steps; he came down a few, and we shook hands. He had a hard, callused hand, very strong grip. "That's a pity. There's a lot of interest in the bridge, what with the tunnel going through and the toll going up." I tried a smile.

Mr. Lithgow's slightly wrinkled but composed features arranged themselves in a corresponding smile. "It's a shame you missed him. I really enjoyed talking to him myself. I'm sure he had a lot of memorabilia; in fact, I know he had. His room's full of it." He gestured above and behind him. "Would you like to see it?"

"Do you think that'd be all right?"

Lithgow retreated a few steps. "I'm sure it would. All he lived for, really. Poor old chap. I'm sure he'd be pleased there was someone taking an interest."

We went up the stairs, past the landing, to the top floor. The light improved a little, coming in through a room with an open door. Lithgow pointed to the closed door opposite. "Stan's room."

"No family or friends to—" I shrugged—"handle his affairs?"

Lithgow opened the door. "Apparently not. Lonely old soul, apart from the members of his society, of course."

"Many of them?"

"A few."

I felt strangely reluctant to go into the dead man's room. I was disconcerted by Lithgow's manner. His clothes weren't expensive, and he wore a slightly shabby air, but he smelled very clean. His voice was clear, and his accent was precise; he sounded old-fashioned rather than well educated, almost as if he'd picked up a set of mannerisms from a play or a book. "Not a member of the society yourself, Mr. Lithgow?"

"Me? Heavens, no. I suppose you're wondering why I'm living in a place like this."

I took out my notebook. "Would you have the names of the society members? Yes, I'm wondering, but you don't have to tell me if you don't want to."

"No objection at all. I'm retired from the public service. Had a lifelong interest in this area. Generations of Lithgows lived here until, well, until I broke the tradition. But now I'm back, and I'm writing a book about the old place. What d'you think of that?"

"Sounds fine to me, Mr. Lithgow. Are you sure about going into Mr. Livermore's room?"

"Of course, of course." He pushed the door wide, and we went into the room. It was rather dark and cold, being on the side of the house away from the sun. A small window let in a little eastern light. It was also obsessively neat and clean. The bed, with a thin gray blanket on top, was made with military precision; all books and papers were set on shelves with aligned edges and right-angled piles. The few personal items on the chest of drawers and bedside table—comb, bus timetable, nail scissors—were clean and carefully laid out.

"An orderly man," I said.

"Very. And a very nice old chap, too. But we all have to go. I just hope I get long enough to do this book. Well, Mr. Kelly, I have my researches to get on with. Take as long as you like. I'm just across the hall if you want me."

He ducked his head and almost bowed himself out of the room. I set about a systematic search, which Stan Livermore's efficient habits made easy. He had a collection of books about the bridge, including those I'd seen in the library, and a good deal of related material—pamphlets, magazine articles, newspaper clippings, and correspondence. What it all came to was an obsession, a fixed idea that the building of the bridge had exacted an enormous toll on lives and happiness. The dislocation and eviction of people from houses on the land resumed for the approaches, the closing of schools and businesses, the diversion of traffic—they all were documented. There was a voluminous recording of the accidents and deaths, and a minute tracing of consequences for wives and families. In the bottom drawer of the chest were files on scores of cases, which ran from medical reports to correspondence with members of Parliament. It all was alphabetical; all the handwriting was clear and legible; all clippings and photographs were annotated with dates and sources. It was too much of a good thing.

I worked through it using the only system I could think of: checking for names. Livermore appeared to have had no special interest in any of the bridge builders. The names came up —Ennis, Madden, Glover, Bradfield—but none was traced beyond the completion of the bridge. There were files on the sixteen men killed, but these petered out in the 1950s, as if twenty years were as long as anyone cared to remember them. The society had devoted itself to getting a suitable memorial for the dead, helping the families of some of the injured men, and attempting to keep people who had worked on the bridge in touch with one another. It seemed a vain task. There was a large bundle of letters returned from the post office marked "Address unknown."

Stan Livermore himself had been a riveter who worked for five years on the job without suffering injury. I found a complimentary reference to Captain David Guthrie, for his intervention in the case of a worker who had been sacked for being asleep on the job. Captain Guthrie had demonstrated that fumes from an ill-maintained piece of equipment had overcome the man, who was reinstated. Casting about, I found no reference to anyone named Tracey or Burton or Lithgow. No Hardys either, or Broadways. I was running out of analytical tools fast and aware that I might be running out of time. Lithgow had given me carte blanche, but that wouldn't cut much ice if Betty Tracey returned and blew my cover. I did a last search for active members of the society as of the latest date and came up with six names. But the last time these individuals and Stan Livermore had convened a meeting was almost a year back. Still, it was something.

As I was tidying up the files, I wondered if

the old men had turned their attention to the new disruption caused by the harbor tunnel: the extra traffic through North Sydney, the noise of the tunneling, the pollution of the harbor. Probably not. Their obsession was with the past, and the people now being plagued by the tunnel builders would have had as much trouble getting a hearing from them as from other Sydneysiders. In a way, it was the same story all over again: The greater good of the greater number, and to hell with the rest.

I left old Stan's room pretty much the way I'd found it and closed the door on his life and his life's work. I'd filled several pages of my notebook and was still riffling through them when I knocked on Lithgow's door.

"Come."

Lithgow's room was in marked contrast with Livermore's; it had two windows, which seemed to let in 200 percent more light and warmth. It was also very untidy. The bed was unmade, and papers and books spilled across from a card table to the bed and onto the floor. Charles Lithgow was sitting on a bentwood chair at the card table, scribbling in a large bound notebook. As in Livermore's room, the bed and chest of drawers were standard issue, but the bright tartan blanket thrown over the bed gave this room a lift. A head, shoulders, and chest photograph of a man in military uniform was set on the chest of drawers at such an angle that the subject seemed to be in a position to survey all four corners of the room.

At my appearance Lithgow pushed back his chair and reached down into a large leather briefcase at his feet. He held up a brown bottle with a yellow label. "Too early for a sherry, Mr. Kelly?"

"When in Rome," I said.

He laughed. "Too true. They start early around here, let me tell you. Not like in the old days, of course, but the traditions linger. I'll just get a glass. Have a seat."

I sat in the only available place, on the bed. The room had very little vacant floor space. Beside the bed was a metal toolbox with the lid open. The few tools, hammer, heavy shifting wrench and lighter spanners, clamps, and screwdrivers seemed appropriate to Lithgow's strong, hard-handed grip. But he was a man of surprises; he got up and moved across the room to where a wine rack had been installed under the window ledge. I could see a dozen or so bottles in place and an elaborate metal and wood corkscrew lying on top of the rack. Lithgow took two squat glasses from the window ledge and polished them with a tissue. He set them on the card table, cleared off the papers he'd been working on, and filled them with sherry from a bottle he selected with great care.

He handed me my glass. "Cheers."

"Thank you." I sipped the very dry sherry. Sherry's not a bad drink; there're hundreds of men in Sydney who'll tell you the same. "Are you a wine buff, Mr. Lithgow?"

"Heavens, no. Perish the thought. I just like a good snort after work or a . . . well, any time appropriate, really. Did you find anything helpful in old Stan's room?"

I sipped some more sherry and turned a page or two in my notebook. "Possibly. No substitute for talking to the man himself, of course. I notice you call him old Stan, as Mrs. Tracey did. Have you been in the house long, Mr. Lithgow?"

"Oh, awhile. Long enough to pick up the local habits, you know."

"Mmm. Were you here on the day he died?"

"I was. Why?"

This was tricky ground. I couldn't reveal that I'd been at the house earlier. My only recourse was to the Betty Tracey ploy again. I grinned. "Mrs. Tracey told me that there was someone else here visiting Mr. Livermore. Another five dollars this cost me. But I suppose she might have meant you."

"No, no." Lithgow sipped his sherry with evident enjoyment. "I was working away. I did talk to old Stan from time to time, but there wasn't much he could tell me, you know. The bridge is terribly important to the history of the area, but it's not the whole story by any means."

I nodded. "He was obsessed, you mean?"

"I'm afraid so. And he had some followers still. In point of fact, they held a little meeting here that day, and a few stayed behind after Stan left to keep his vigil. I think one of them might have arrived too late to see Stan. They're old, you see, and not always too sure of the time."

"You know about that, the bridge at sunset thing?"

"Oh, yes. Now look, I don't want you to think I'm a terrible snooper, I'm not. But I do keep a diary, and I did provide them with a bottle of sherry." He held up his glass so that the light shone through the clear, pale liquid. "Not this stuff, of course."

I was leaning forward eagerly, too eagerly. I tried to transfer the enthusiasm to the sherry, holding up my own glass to the light and taking a long sip. "It is very good. Do you mean you know the names of the men who were here that day?"

"Yes, I believe so. Why? Is it important?"

I improvised fast. "Well, one of them will probably become the head of the society now, wouldn't you say? If I can talk to him, I can still do the story as planned."

Lithgow frowned and drank some more sherry. "Yes. See what you mean. Just a minute. I should have the names in my diary. Poor old chaps, quite mad, you know. Quite mad."

18

WHILE HE WAS RUMMAGING IN HIS PAPERS, I STOOD UP AND TOOK A LOOK OUT THE window. I hadn't seen it at first because of the way the light fell on the glass, but the view of the bridge was breathtaking. The structure seemed to rise up almost beneath my feet, and to dominate the near and far distance.

"Wonderful, isn't it?" Lithgow said. "One of the reasons I took the room."

"It sure is." I turned away from the window. "How're you doing there?"

He seemed to have difficulty tearing his eyes away from the view. "Oh, I'm pretty sure I can turn it up. Hold on a minute. Another sherry?"

I shook my head and tried to curb my impatience. For all I knew, Betty Tracey might stay in some pub all day, or she might've gone to the shop for a packet of tea. I noticed a large

225

mug sitting on the floor near where Lithgow had been working. It was red-rimmed inside. *Soup and sherry*, I thought. *Well, it's his stomach.* I examined the photograph on Lithgow's chest of drawers. There was a strong family resemblance. The soldier had the same broad, high forehead and wide jaw. His face, like Lithgow's, looked almost too big for the shoulders. Same light eyes and relaxed expression. Lieutenant Lithgow, 1st Australian Imperial Force. Several campaign ribbons, carefully tinted by the photographer.

"My father," Lithgow said. "He was at Gallipoli and the Somme."

"I had a grandfather did the same," I said. "Then he went off and got himself killed in the North Russia campaign. How'd your father come out of it all?"

"Were you in the army yourself?"

I nodded. "Malaya. You?"

Lithgow didn't reply. He held up a card. "Here we are. The date was the twelfth, right?"

"That sounds right."

"Stan had three visitors: Perce Templeton, Harry Case, and Merv Dent. With old Stan himself, I think that made up the whole of the society."

I wrote the names down, trying not to seem overly anxious. "They were still here when Stan left?"

"I think so. Yes."

"Uh-huh. Well, I wonder which of them I should see. You say one arrived late. Maybe the least keen. One of the others'd be more likely to go into the chair, wouldn't you say?"

"I really don't know."

"Who was the late one?"

Lithgow shrugged. "I couldn't say."

"Never mind. This is very helpful, Mr. Lithgow. You wouldn't have any addresses, would you?"

Lithgow examined his card. "I believe Messrs. Templeton and Case live at a retirement village in Gladesville. Mr. Dent lives somewhere hereabouts. I've used him as a source. Let me see." He went back to rummaging. "Ah, yes. Twenty-two Windmill Lane."

I made notes. There was a drop or two left in my sherry glass. I drained them and put the glass down in front of the portrait of the soldier. "Many thanks, Mr. Lithgow. Big help." I found myself imitating his clipped speech. Definitely time to go. We shook hands, and he ushered me out as far as the landing.

I went down the stairs and out the front door quickly. No Betty Tracey in sight. A few curious faces at the louver windows, but no problems. I went to my car and located Windmill Lane in the *Gregory's*. It was a short stroll away. It was a fair bet that the pair who lived in Gladesville arrived together; that made it likely that Dent, who lived close by, was the late one. That was consistent with human nature. The late one was the most likely to have heard me talking to Betty Tracey. I knew I was drawing a long bow. Maybe the man I'd seen enter a house ahead of me in Pump Street on my first visit hadn't entered 43A; maybe he hadn't noticed me at all. Maybe he wasn't Merv Dent. Maybe Stan Livermore had simply fallen and hit his head. I took out my notes and checked through the list of names of men injured in the bridge construction. All three names Lithgow had given me appeared. I shoved the directory back in the glove box, locked the car, and headed for Windmill Lane.

At the top of Pump Street I got another angle on the bridge, different from the view from Lithgow's window. Now it looked less impressive, as if it were too big for the job it was doing. The water it spanned didn't seem to need such massive engineering to master it. Still, it was always going to be more interesting than the tunnel. I thought I could see a yellow stain in the water in the area where the tunneling work was going on. But that might have been my antitunnel imagination at work. A few yards down the steep street, and the water and bridge disappeared.

Windmill Street had probably never looked so good before in its long history. The houses had been cleaned up and repainted in colonial colors, the new paving was in keeping with the buildings, and something green was growing in almost every place it was possible for something green to grow. The harmony was putting me in the wrong mood. I was possibly about to face a multiple killer, a man with an obsession that was stronger to him than the claims of human life, a twisted individual. We're all twisted, but some twists are more dangerous than others. . . . I was trying to build up some aggression. I should have had the taste of tobacco and beer in my mouth, not good dry sherry.

As I turned into Windmill Lane, I realized that my attitude was mainly one of curiosity rather than anger. I had questions rather than accusations. What forces could prompt a man to kill repeatedly? Why had he waited so long to begin killing, or *had* he waited? The cases of death and disappearance I was confronting now—were they only the tip of an iceberg? How had the executions been managed, and what justifications would the executioner have? The lane was cobblestoned in the same way as the area behind the houses in Pump Street. But here the worn-down stones were firmly set, and the gutters had been renewed where years of running water had eaten away the stone. One side of the lane was completely taken up by a succession of brick fences of varying heights. Gardening had been going on here, too. The fences were covered in leafless wisteria and other vines.

The houses were on the other side, facing toward the water. Cute, narrow terraces, very scrubbed up, with brass knockers and painted wrought iron. There were ten houses in the lane, numbering from 1 to 10. There was no number 22, and this part of the Rocks had been untouched by developer or restorer. There never had been a number 22.

As I rechecked the numbering of the houses in the lane and the streets at either end, certain impressions and recollections began to come together in my mind. Now that I was out of his presence, I felt some disturbing familiarity about Charles Lithgow that I hadn't felt when I was with him. It was as if I'd met him before in another context, and the remeeting had blotted this out. I struggled to remember, to place the feeling, and failed. But I started to walk quickly back to Pump Street. Had I been conned? Had it all been too easy? Something else about Lithgow disturbed me. Some irritant, something not quite right. But I couldn't locate it.

I reentered number 43A by the back, went through the porch bedroom into the kitchen and almost fell as my feet tangled with something on the floor. I steadied myself by grabbing the doorjamb and looked down. Betty Tracey was lying on the floor. The back of her head was a dark, pulpy mess. Her gray hair was stained a dark color near the crown and was streaked dark red for the rest of its untidy length. I felt for signs of life at her wrist and neck the way I had with Stan Livermore and got the same result. The little woman's head was turned around so that she seemed almost to be looking back over her shoulder. She was even more twisted and hunched in death than she had been in life.

I straightened up and moved quickly to the stairs. All quiet topside. I went up and saw that the doors to both Livermore's and Lithgow's rooms were open. Old Stan's room had been gone through, quickly but by someone who knew what was where. Most of the files were missing, along with some of the books and photographs. In Lithgow's room almost nothing remained apart from the furniture and the wine rack. The papers, books, photographs, toolbox, and other things I'd remarked all were gone. I pulled out the drawers and opened the cupboards. They were empty but might always have been so. The wastepaper basket, which I now remembered as being crammed with paper, was empty and lying on its side. There was almost nothing of Mr Lithgow remaining, except his soup mug, sherry glasses, and wine rack, which contained ten bottles, none of which would sell for less than twenty dollars.

There was no way of sliding out of this one: My fingerprints were in the house, my car had been parked in the street for an hour or more, and I'd been seen at the place previously. Besides, I didn't want to make an anonymous phone call about Betty Tracey. She might have been an old sharpster, but she deserved more than that. I'd seen a killer and could identify him, although I'd have laid a hundred to one now that his name wasn't Lithgow or anything like it. I found the house telephone in Mrs. Tracey's dark, musty front room and called the police. While I waited for them to come, I did another quick search of Livermore's and Lithgow's rooms. Nothing in old Stan's. In the other room I found a pair of socks that had been left under the bed. Handy if you were a sniffer dog. I gave the blankets a twitch and something dark and soft fell to the floor. The object was a woolen glove. For no good reason, I sniffed it. It smelled of the sea. For me, smell triggers recall better than any of the other senses. I remembered where I'd seen Charles Lithgow before.

The cops who came must have been reading the papers and going to community policing class. They treated me with extreme gentleness, showed consideration to the older neighbors who were alarmed by the arrival of an ambulance and another police car, and listened patiently to an abbreviated version of my story. The second car brought two detectives, who talked briefly to the uniformed men. I sat on the stairs, feeling drained, tired of the stink of the house, light-headed.

One of the detectives showed me his card. "Campbell," he said.

I rubbed my face and felt the hardness of the scabs that had formed over my scratches. "Fine Scots name, Campbell," I said. "I'm Irish myself, mostly."

"Have you been drinking, Mr. Hardy?"

I held up my thumb and forefinger, an inch apart. "A tiny sherry."

"I think you'd better come with us. Do you have a vehicle?"

I handed him the keys. "Blue Falcon across the street. Don't put any dings in it, or I'll sue."

"Do you have a weapon, Mr. Hardy?"

I held my jacket open. "Your blokes took it away from me a couple of nights ago. If I go quietly, d'you think you might give it back?"

"Just sit quietly there a minute, sir. We're waiting for the technical people. When they come, we can go."

I said, "The Campbells a'comin'."

"What?"

"Nothing, Sergeant. Don't take offense."

Campbell made a grunting sound and turned away from me. He nodded conspiratorially to his partner, and for a moment they and the uniformed policemen all stood in the narrow hallway, like train travelers for whom there were no seats. Two men in white coats walked through the front door. The cops all sprang into action.

"Photos, dusting, bagging, blood samples, all the usual things," Campbell said.

One of the white coats mock tugged his forelock. "Sir," he said.

"Don't be funny, Simmo. I'm not in the mood." Campbell crooked a finger at me. "Mr. Hardy."

I got up and moved toward the door. I took the glove from my pocket and handed it to the white coat. "This is a glove worn by the killer, Simmo," I said. "You probably should check it for fingerprints."

I was laughing fit to burst as Campbell and his mate hustled me through the door and into their car.

19

I TOLD PARTS OF THE STORY TO CAMPBELL IN THE CAR, MORE TO HIM AND ANOTHER cop in a cold, bare interview room at the Sydney police station in Central Street, and the rest of it to an inspector and Ralph Wren in another more comfortable room in the same building. It smelled of paint; all police stations these days seemed to smell of paint and renovation. We sat on plastic chairs around a conference table with places for another eight participants. Wren had a batch of papers with him; the inspector and I had nothing.

Wren, a small, dark man with a prominent nose and a nervous sniff, took notes. When I finished talking, he looked up and sniffed. "Concealing evidence," he said.

"What are you talking about?"

"The bodies in the harbor."

"I'd say I discovered evidence or revealed it or something. I didn't conceal it. If I'd hauled the stiffs up, you would have done me for unlicensed salvaging."

The bulky, bald-headed inspector, whose name was Lucas or Loomis (Wren had muttered the introduction) grinned, but Wren's face didn't change. "You're too smart for your own good, Hardy. You're in trouble here."

"I don't think so, Wren. You're forgetting something."

"What?"

"I didn't see inside that canvas. Could be dead cats for all I know."

"Is this the point?" Lucas or Loomis said. "We can sort all that out later. What about this Lithgow? You've seen him twice now, Mr. Hardy. At close quarters." I nodded. I'd told them about my first meeting with Lithgow— on the water under the bridge. The smell on the glove had brought the memory back. Lithgow was the man in the boat made for sailing and rowing who'd hailed us and offered help. It all fitted: the view of the bridge from his window, the callused hands, his hesitation in saying when he liked a drink. My guess was that what he had almost said was "After a good sail or a row."

Wren flicked back through his notes and looked at a computer printout sheet he'd brought along with him. "Your theory is that he killed Mrs. Tracey because she might be able to identify him?"

"Right," I said. "And Stan Livermore for much the same reason."

Wren gave a sniff and tapped the sheet. "You didn't mention any of this when you made a statement at Woolloomooloo a couple of days ago."

"Come on, Ralph," the inspector said. He was ten years older than I was, close to twenty older than Wren, and he used his rank and the age differential like a heavier champ using his weight against a contender. "Let's stick to the point. First thing is to pull up those bodies, if that's what they are."

"Water police," Wren said. "Cheeky bastards."

"And you'll have to take me along to identify the spot," I said. "Sorry, Mr. Wren, Mr. Lucas."

"Loomis. Are you sure you're up to it, Mr. Hardy? You seemed a bit unsteady back there a while ago."

Loomis was smarter than Wren, and he knew it. He'd just managed to tone down my insolence. "I'll be all right," I said.

"Good." Loomis rubbed his hands together. "Think I'll leave you the paperwork, Ralph, and take a turn on the water myself. Get on the blower to the floaties, will you? And, Ralph, we don't want any reporters or cameras. Got me?"

Wren left the room, and Loomis escorted me to the canteen, where we drank coffee and ate surprisingly good toasted sandwiches. He was a relaxed and pleasant man, and I felt myself relaxing in his company. I realized that I'd been wound up tight; Loomis knew it. He blew on the surface of his coffee and waved to a colleague across the room.

"How's Meredith?" I said.

"Doing well. I heard you called in on him the other day."

"He saved my bloody life. You know about the Tobin thing?"

He nodded. I guessed that crooked cops, former and current, weren't his favorite people. "This is a bizarre case. The bridge has been up for nearly sixty years. Why would anyone suddenly take it into his mind to start killing the sons of the builders?"

I shook my head. "Answer that, and you've got him."

"You've got no clues, you say."

"Too many bloody clues. One way and another you can put together quite a list of the people killed or seriously injured on the job. It'd run to a hundred, maybe more. Someone connected with one of those people is the most likely candidate. It's before the migrants came here and started doing all the hard yakka, remember. They have names like Smith and Jones."

Loomis drank some coffee gloomily. "People who take phony names often don't use their imagination. You've got a list like that, have you?"

"Partial only."

"Any names like Goulburn or Bathurst on it?"

"I don't remember. My notes're in my car."

"Hang on. More coffee?" I shook my head, and the inspector went across to a wall phone. He spoke briefly into it, got more coffee for himself at the counter, and returned. "Your car's in the basement. I've taken the liberty of asking an officer to bring us your notes."

"You're buying the food."

He drank some more coffee and relaxed in his chair. "If this breaks the way we think it will, it's going to be a big story. How much of it do you want, Hardy? What's the extent of your interest?"

"Doesn't extend very far," I said. "I'd like to be able to handle my client's identification of her father, if it's him down there, before any of the media get hold of it. That's about it. I'd like to feel that Meredith got his share of the credit for the detective work. I took my lead from his interest in missing persons cases with a bridge connection. He was on the right track."

"Fair enough. More than fair. The trouble is, there's not going to be much credit to spread around unless we catch the killer."

"That's your department. I was hired to find someone. It looks as if I've done it."

"It does, it does. Ah, here we are."

A female constable appeared at Loomis's elbow. She ignored me and handed him my notebook and accompanying bits of paper.

Loomis lifted his bum off the seat in gentlemanly fashion. "Thank you, Constable."

The policewoman said, "Yes, sir," turned smartly, and left the canteen.

"Can't get used to it," Loomis said. "Especially the guns. Well, let's see what we have here." He spread the papers out, sorting them rapidly and efficiently. His hands alighted on the photocopies. "Lists of names. Christ!" It was the first aroused response I'd seen from him. I leaned forward and saw that he was looking at the blotchy, grainy photocopy of the picture of the riveter doing his stuff on a narrow ledge a couple of hundred feet up.

"Scary," I said.

"Mmm." Loomis ran his eye down the list I'd copied from the Veterans of the Bridge pamphlet. "See what you mean. Smith and Jones. Nothing . . ."

"Geographical?"

"Right." He pushed the papers across to me. I patted them into some sort of order and put them in my pocket. "It's got to be someone who only recently found out that he had a grievance or only recently acquired the means to do something about it."

I was impressed. "Death notices early this year. Match 'em up with the names of the dead and injured."

"Slow and messy. Have you considered that there could be other people under threat?"

"Of course I have. What about Paul Guthrie? *His* father helped to build the bloody thing."

Loomis shook his head. "From what you've told us, this nut has singled out the actual construction phase. Still, you could be right. You evidently admire Guthrie, feel some responsibility to him. Does that affect your position?"

I munched on a last crust from my toasted ham and cheese sandwich and swilled down some cold coffee. It was midafternoon. Too early for a drink, but I'd have succumbed if one had been available. "How d'you mean, Inspector?" I said.

"Are you really trying, Hardy? Do you want to stop this maniac? Aren't you embarrassed about the way he fooled you? Watched you while you looked under the bridge?"

"That's a point," I said. "He's a bridge freak. Rows on the harbor. You've got the manpower to look into those things. I haven't."

"Sent you off on a wild-goose chase? Diverted you while he cleaned up his room and bashed an old woman to death?"

I stared at him. "What do you want me to do?"

His high forehead wrinkled. The wrinkles ran all the way up to where his hairline used to be and beyond. This was deep thought being demonstrated. I was aware of a growing hostility between us. "How about this dinghy, sailboat, or whatever he was in?"

"What about it?"

"Did it have a name, for Christ's sake?"

"I thought of that, Inspector."

"And?"

"I didn't notice."

"Some detective," Loomis said.

We boarded the water police launch at the pontoon dock I'd seen during my previous excursion on the water. Loomis exerted his heavy charm on the uniformed sergeant and two constables running the boat and also spread it around the two frogmen, who jiggled and slapped their hands together as if they could hardly wait to get out of this unnatural environment and into their true habitat. They had lights similar to the one Ray Guthrie had used but stronger-looking, and one of them had a waterproof tool kit at his feet. Loomis took a careful look around before giving the signal to move out toward the bridge.

"I don't see any reporters or camera crews, do you, Hardy?"

It was an olive branch of a sort; we'd hardly spoken since the police station. Loomis had concentrated on making efficient arrangements, and I'd worked on steeling myself for something nasty. "Looks clear to me," I said. "This shouldn't take long. I'm told it's only fifteen meters deep."

Loomis smiled. "Is that all? Christ, look at the muck in the water."

I guided the launch out to what Ray had called the dead set middle. The water was being chopped up by a light breeze, and it was cold on the deck. Loomis had brought along a heavy police overcoat; I was still in my shirt and jacket; unless we got it over with quickly, I was going to be shivering. "Here. And I think what you're looking for is over in that direction."

The frogmen nodded, pulled down their masks, and went over the side. One of the constables handed down the tool kit.

"Rather them than me," Loomis said.

I nodded. "My mate needed a half hour shower afterward. And some brandy. Wouldn't have anything with you, Inspector?"

Loomis didn't reply. A ferry passed us, and a few curious passengers watched our boat as it tossed lightly in the wake. One of them flicked a cigarette butt into the water, and Loomis glared. "I'd like to make him jump in and fish it out. To answer your question, there's bound to be a drop of something aboard for medicinal reasons. If we need it, we'll get it."

A couple of sailing boats gave us a wide berth, the way cars keep clear of police cars on the road, and a rubber boat with a powerful outboard skipped past on the north side. There was a constant hum of traffic noise, road and rail, from the bridge. After what seemed like an hour but was probably only half that, one of the frogmen surfaced and signaled. The launch edged toward him, and the cops ran a line over the side. The frogman went under again, and we waited. The line quivered, and the sergeant pressed a button on the electric winch. The line tightened and came in slowly and steadily. The constables moved to the side, with heavy gloves on their hands and hooks and lengths of plastic rope at the ready.

The water broke and a dripping gray-green package came to the surface. It was about six feet long, sealed at both ends. A length of chain hung from one end, free of the line which the frogmen had wound around it. The policemen lifted the bundle over the side and laid it on the deck. Water and a greeny black goo flowed from inside it. I expected a smell of some kind, but there wasn't any. Loomis stepped back, but not quickly enough to avoid the water splashing over his shoes.

"Shit!" He took out a handkerchief and blew his nose. "Get on with it, Sergeant. And don't let's forget the anchors. What are they, Hardy? Oil drums?"

I was staring at the canvas package and the chain and thinking of burials at sea, honorable and dishonorable deaths—floggings and keel-haulings. It all felt like a step back into history, back beyond the time of the building of the bridge, back to the beginnings. I shivered, and not because of the cold. "Yeah," I said, "oil drums, recycled."

Loomis gave a short laugh and bent to examine the canvas. He straightened up and wiped his face with the back of his hand. "Not much we can do with this. Must be hundreds of places sell canvas like that. Same with the chain. Would you say this Lithgow was a bright bloke?"

"Very."

Loomis sighed. "That's not going to help."

The frogmen and other cops worked hard and efficiently. They got four canvas bundles and four concrete plugs the size of a couple of house bricks from the bottom. Loomis watched the operation sourly; he turned his collar up against the wind and rubbed his hands together. When the last dive and lift were complete, the senior frogman pulled up his mask.

"That's it, Inspector."

"Thanks. See any weapons down there?"

The frogman shook his head. "The bottom's like all silty and soft. Those plugs had really settled in. Whoever put them down there knew what he was doing."

Loomis scarcely heard him. He was looking toward the quay, where a group of people had assembled. "Bugger it," Loomis said. "We've been spotted. Where do we dock, Sergeant?"

"Harris Street, sir. Wharf twenty-five."

"Anywhere else we could go?"

"Sans Souci?"

Loomis shook his head. "Just get us there as fast as you can. And get on the radio and tell them not to let any press near the wharf. Can you do that?"

The sergeant almost saluted and hurried forward to the cabin. The launch's engines roared into life, and we churned the water as we moved fast toward the bridge. We passed under it, and I felt the massive structure above me like a heavy, gray iron cloud, blotting out the pale afternoon sun. "What now?" I said.

Loomis hunched his shoulders inside the heavy coat. "Nothing nice," he said. "We open up and take a look. Then we ask their nearest and dearest to do the same. Got any idea what they'll look like, Hardy?"

I shook my head. "You?"

"I've seen a few floaters in my time. Mostly banged about by whoever killed them and by the rocks. It's not pretty. But all wrapped up like this? I don't know."

The launch changed course and the canvas-wrapped bodies moved a little on the deck, as if protesting about being raised from their cold, wet graves.

20

"DO YOU WANT TO BE ON HAND FOR THIS, HARDY?" LOOMIS SMOKED A THIN CIGAR as we watched the bodies and their anchors being unloaded at the police dock.

"What happens now?"

"Pathologist's on the way. We'll open 'em up and take a look. See what the identification possibilities are. After that, autopsy and inquests and the rest of the circus. Any idea how long they've been down there?"

I shrugged. "Meredith's probably got the longest missing one in his files. You'd better ask Wren."

Loomis nodded and blew smoke out toward the water. We were standing behind a glass shelter a little back from the dock. The light had faded, and everything around was taking on the gray color of the canvas bundles. "Better phone him. If I know Ralph, he won't have anything to do with this side of things."

"Frank Parker said he was a good man, Wren."

"He is. Good deskman. Tireless. D'you want a smoke?"

"No, thanks. Have you got a bucket on you?"

Loomis laughed. "Some tough guy."

But an hour later it was me who was standing inside the room where the bundles had been unwrapped and Inspector Loomis who was away somewhere retching his guts up.

The pathologist, Dr. Carstairs, was a slim, handsome type who looked too young to be having anything to do with death. That impression vanished as soon as he opened his mouth; his voice was rough-edged and unemotional. "Get cracking, Mr. Bennett."

Carstairs buttoned up his white coat and pulled on rubber gloves. His assistant, evidently named Bennett, did the same, and Carstairs signaled to him to use bolt cutters on the chain and a knife on the stitching of the canvas. The bundles had been neatly sewn along one side in big, strong stitches. "No telling," Carstairs said. "Gas from the bodies is the story here. Could swell up and burst, in which case you'll have guts and muck all over the place, or it could go the other way: Gas could be absorbed and the body would shrivel."

Loomis nodded, still very tough. "What decides that, Doctor?"

"State of the body when living: age, condition, last meal, and manner of death."

The assistant was still working on the chains. Nothing yet. "What are the chances of identification in both cases?" I said.

"Difficult, either way. Not like with a buried corpse. There, as you'd know, Inspector, the bacteria in the earth get to work and you get putrefaction pretty quickly and destruction of the tissue. Lots of crawly things around to help. Here you'll get preservation of the tissue because the only active bacteria are in the body. But there'll be mold and such. Parts of the face could stick to the canvas. We'll see."

Bennett got the chains off and went to work on the stitching. The bundles were lying on two wide metal tables, which were already awash with water and other matter leaking from inside. The room we were in had a concrete floor and bare walls, artificial light. It smelled strongly of disinfectant, which was starting to be overlain by the smell of seawater and something else. Bennett cut the stitches of each bundle in turn and pulled aside the seam on the first.

The creature inside looked like a mummy, scarcely larger than child size. It was naked, shrunken, and a greeny black color. There was no hair on its head. As the pathologist had predicted, parts of the flesh seemed to have formed a mold on the canvas and came away when the material was pulled back. An exposed shoulder bone was white.

"Jesus," Loomis said, "he looks a hundred years old."

Carstairs nodded. "Absorption of the gas, as I said. Wasn't young when he died. Bald, stooped possibly, arthritic, I'd say . . ." He leaned over and peered closely at the shrunken head and the clawlike hands. He straightened up and looked at me. "Dentition intact and a ring on the third finger of the left hand. Shouldn't be too much trouble with identification."

I nodded. I didn't know whether to feel relieved or alarmed that the corpse bore no possible resemblance to Brian Madden. Before we moved on to the next one, I noticed that the fingernails and toenails on the shriveled body were long and curling.

"Dr. Carstairs?" Bennett said. He'd pulled back part of the canvas and stopped. There was a smell now, all right—of old meat and old milk and rotten eggs and everything else bad you can think of. Carstairs waved to Bennett to continue, and he tugged the canvas apart. The mess was like a dozen or more squirming, green-black, half-skinned rabbits. The corpse had ruptured, and the organs were splattered around and twisted together. The man had been big; his limbs and torso were still sufficiently defined to be able to see that, and he had a massive head, which lolled drunkenly as if it had been half wrenched from the shoulders.

"Broken neck," Carstairs said, "and massive gas formation in the gut. Mr. Loomis?"

But Loomis had run for the door, his shoulders heaving. Carstairs looked at the closing door with amusement. I looked up at the ceiling and drew a breath. This wasn't Madden either. "This is the best argument I've ever seen for cremation," I said.

Carstairs snorted as we watched Bennett resume snipping. "You seem remarkably composed, Mr.?"

"Hardy. I can stand it. I've seen the insides of men before, Doctor. I've seen them holding themselves together, literally."

"Ah, a soldier. Tell me, which is worse? This or combat wounds?"

"I don't know," I said. "It's all bad."

"That one had been in the water longest, at a guess. It's going to be very interesting sorting all this out. We have a serial killer here, do we?"

"Yes. Pretty unusual."

Carstairs examined the black tongue protruding from the crazily angled head. "Here it is, yes. I spent a couple of years in New York. Different story there."

The next corpse was intact and less shriveled than the first, though it had gone through the same process. The legs were drawn up toward the abdomen, and the arms had locked in a rigid position across the chest. Naked and green-black like the others, Brian Madden had for some reason retained more dignity. Under the harsh light his body looked like a three-dimensional rubbing taken from the tomb of a medieval saint. The wet, matted hair lay on the skull like a metal cap; his eyes were closed, and his mouth had set in a line that was almost a smile.

"How did he die, Doctor?"

Carstairs ran his eye over the body. "Can't say. No obvious signs of violence. Time will tell. You're going?"

I was on my way to the door. "I said I could stand it. I didn't say I enjoyed it."

I rang Louise Madden in Leura and told her that I'd found her father, and how and where.

I had to wait a long time before she responded. "How did he die, Mr. Hardy?"

"We don't know. All I can tell you is that there were no signs of violence on the body. We'll have to wait. I would've come to see you, but there's no time."

"What do you mean?"

"This'll be a big story. No way of avoiding that. I thought you should get the news from me first. It's not much, but—"

"Thank you. My dad was a very private person. He wouldn't like being part of a—a mass killing." Her voice broke on the word. "Will I have to identify him?"

"I'm not sure, under the circumstances. I'm in touch with the police, and I'll let you know. Will you be all right? Do you have a friend or someone to stay with?"

"I've got plenty of friends. I'll be all right."

"I mean, someone who can protect you. And you should contact the Leura police and ask them to keep an eye on things."

"I don't understand."

"Look, Louise, this man is insane. We don't know where he's going to stop."

"It sounds as if you know who he is."

"It's complicated. I talked to him. I didn't know at the time that he was responsible."

"Has he killed people other than . . . like my dad?"

"Yes, he has."

"Then you should worry about yourself. If he knows you, he might . . ."

"I can take care of myself. I don't want to alarm you. I can't see how he could find out that you employed me, but you never know. Just be careful. And I'm very sorry that it turned out like this. If there's anything else I can do, just ask."

"I'll manage. And thank you, thank you. It's better to know."

"That's right."

I hung up and turned my attention to the scotch I'd poured before making the call. She was right. It *was* better to know. The most painracked faces I'd seen were the people I'd reported negative results to: no sign of father, daughter, son, mother. And she was right about my exposure. If Lithgow had seen my car, he could trace me. He might even have heard me give my name to Betty Tracey. Had I given it? I couldn't remember. If he only knew it, now was the time to come after me if that was what he was going to do. I was dead tired, and there wasn't so much as a pea rifle in the house.

The newshounds had been busy all night. A connection had been made between the salvage operation under the bridge and the tight security at the police dock. The coming and going of the pathologist had been observed, and something had been gleaned from a call to his office. Somebody had leaked something about Colin Glover, and the bloodhounds were on the trail. Loomis turned the handling of the press over to Wren, who straight-batted for as long as he could, which wasn't long. They got to Clyde Glover, and the name Barclay came up. A fresh scent. By the late TV news a thin, speculative story was forming. Wren was confronted with a wild hypothesis that spoke of mass suicides as a result of some scandal involving the building of the bridge. He had no recourse but to tell the truth. The morning headlines read: CURSE OF THE BRIDGE and BRIDGE KILLER SOUGHT. The afternoon tabloids wouldn't be so restrained. Some cop had leaked my name to the reporters. I was described as an "enquiry agent."

I learned all this from Loomis and Wren, who called me to a morning conference at St. Vincents during which we could get ten minutes with Meredith. We talked briefly in the lobby before being escorted upstairs. Wren told me that he had driven my car to the hospital and that it needed work on the clutch. He handed me the keys.

"Thanks," I said. "How is he?" I asked Loomis.

"Strong as a bull. He'll be back. You know, Hardy, it'll do his prospects a lot of good if we can catch this loony."

"I know."

"And stop him," Wren said. "He hasn't killed only the sons of engineers."

I said, "Right."

We followed the bustling nurse down the corridor. She gestured for us to stop and went into the room alone. Loomis leaned against the wall. "Tobin's none too happy with you."

"Been out to see him, have you?"

Loomis flushed. "Watch it! Tobin's a piece of shit to me. Always was. I only meant—"

"You only meant that I've got enemies and should have as many policeman friends as possible. I get the message, Inspector."

The nurse beckoned us in, and we arranged ourselves on chairs around the bed. Meredith was propped up on pillows. There were no tubes into his head, just one into his arm and one into the body. His color was good.

"Hell, Lloyd," Loomis said, "you look better than I feel."

Meredith nodded. "Inspector, Ralph, Hardy. It's good to see you." He touched the newspaper on the bed. "I was right about the bridge being the link."

"You were," Loomis said. "It was good work."

"And we still want your input," Wren said.

Loomis filled Meredith in on details that hadn't made it into the papers, mostly about my role. The news stories hadn't mentioned me, and that was fine: Being a high-public-profile private detective would be like playing football in pink shorts.

"Fingerprints in Lithgow's room?" Meredith asked.

Loomis nodded. "Plenty. But no matchups."

"The canvas and the plugs?"

"Undergoing analysis," Wren said.

Meredith rubbed his face, which was smooth-shaven. They'd washed and combed his hair, too. He looked almost ready to go back to work. "He told Hardy he'd retired from the public service?"

"Which almost certainly means," Loomis said, "that he was never in the bloody public service."

"What then?" Wren said.

I shrugged. "Small business, maybe. To do with boats. Just a guess."

"Great." Loomis sat back in his chair, took out a thin cigar, and ran it between his fingers. "This is one of the biggest harbor cities in the world. Any idea how many small businesses to do with boats there'd be?"

Meredith smiled. "The seafood restaurants alone."

Loomis and I both laughed, but Wren

looked grim. "I don't see what there is to be amused about. This man has killed seven people, maybe more. We don't know who he is, where he lives, or anything about him except that he talks politely and can row a boat. I'd call this a major problem case."

"Easy, Ralph," Loomis said. "No use blowing the boiler. Any bright ideas, Hardy?"

"What about the victims? If they all were oldest sons of bridge men, that could narrow the field of possible future targets. At least they could be located and protected."

Wren shook his head. "Two of them weren't oldest sons. There's lots of them. Not as many as sons of men killed or injured on the bridge, but still too many to cover."

"There has to be a reason why he just started this up recently," Meredith said.

Wren checked his notes. "Fits with retirement. Time and money to track down and kill people."

"That boat of his looked expensive. He didn't seem like a man to whom time and money were a big problem," I said. "I should've picked up on that at the time, but I didn't. There were other odd things about him, too."

"Like what?" Wren snapped.

I shook my head, trying to locate the source of the disquiet, the feeling that something I'd seen had been wrong. I couldn't do it. "I don't know. Can't put my finger on it."

Meredith was suddenly looking tired. He

blinked a few times and slid down on his pillows. "The other possibility is that he found something out recently, something that triggered all this. Have there been any out-of-the-usual stories about the bridge in the last six months?"

"Bloody toll and tunnel's all I can think of." Loomis grunted.

Wren made a note. "We can check it."

Loomis smoothed the wrapping on his cigar. "Any more bright ideas, Lloyd?"

Meredith glanced at me. "Only one."

I looked at the man who had saved my life and had taken two bullets the shooter would have been happy to have put in me. He had two tubes running out of him, and all the energy and enthusiasm he would usually be exerting with his body were concentrated in the challenging look in his eyes. Our ten minutes were almost up. "I thought you'd never ask," I said.

21

RALPH WREN GOT BUSY, AND HE HAD VERY RECEPTIVE MEDIA TO DEAL WITH. HARBOR
bridge stories, apparently, rate just below
quins and bimbos for ratings and newspaper
sales, and what Wren served up was swallowed
whole: BRIDGE KILLER INSANE, SAYS EXPERT was one
headline. An unnamed psychologist hypothe-
sized that the person responsible for the
deaths of the bridge builders' sons was "moti-
vated by an irrational hatred of the bridge,
which was undoubtedly a symbol for a deep
sexual uncertainty." The article went on to
compare the killer to assorted psychopaths
distinguished by sexual confusion and clini-
cally tested low intelligence.

A television report laid stress on the magnificent achievement of Bradfield, Ennis, Barclay, Glover, and the others. It showed old,

flickering black-and-white footage of the building and opening of the bridge and emphasized the safety and stability of the structure. "No one will ever sing 'The harbor bridge is falling down,'" the voice-over commentary ran, "and no one has ever disputed that the bridge is worth every cent and every drop of sweat it cost." The report concluded with the statement that "the serial killer is offering an insult to the memories of great men and an affront to all Australians who care about their country's history."

This went on for two days. The killer was described as "probably impotent and mother-fixated," the bridge builders as "heroes," and their families as "devastated." The artist's drawing of Lithgow was circulated, but it had been modified to make him look brutish and humorless. The usual number of crank calls and letters were received by the police and the media, and several of the more inane and perverted of these received some publicity. The outstanding war records of some of the builders' offspring, male and female, got a mention. This was at my suggestion. There was something about the photograph of Lithgow's father, and his reaction when the topic of war came up, that worked in my mind like a stone in a shoe. But I still couldn't make sense of it.

Ray Guthrie was interviewed by the police but not troubled further. Louise Madden was not required to identify her father. My recognition plus dental records and the presence of a scar from a minor operation on Madden's right knee was sufficient. The autopsy revealed that he had died from a blow to the temple, which had caused a massive hemorrhage.

"That would have been quick and probably painless," I told Louise. She was finishing off the job in Castlecrag, and I'd driven out there to give her the news in person.

She used a mallet to knock a heavy stone into place in a rockery she'd constructed. "That's good. When can I bury him?"

"Soon, I should think."

"Will you come?"

"If you want me to."

She nodded and swung the mallet again. The dull thwacks reminded me of the sounds Helen Broadway made when she staked vines on her husband's land. I'd pleaded with her to leave him, and she wouldn't. I'd pulled up some of the vines, and we'd shouted at each other. Louise Madden stopped working and stared at me. "What's wrong?"

"Nothing." I shook my head to clear the images.

"This isn't over for you, Cliff, is it?"

"Not really. Not until he's caught."

"And what's happening on that front?"

The police and I anticipated that Lithgow would have read my name in the press and put two and two together.

"We're waiting," I said.

* * *

Lithgow called on the third night. I was in my office.

"You know who this is?" he said.

"Yes." I switched on the police-provided recording equipment. There was a similar hookup at home.

"I realize you'll be recording this, Mr. Hardy. I'm not stupid, you see?"

There was nothing to say to that, and I didn't try.

"I want you to go out to a telephone box in William Street—the one opposite the Metropolitan Hotel. Have you got that?"

"Yes. When?"

"Now, and don't contact the police or bring anyone with you when we meet."

"We're meeting, are we?" He hung up without answering, and I replaced the receiver thoughtfully. I didn't really want to go up against Lithgow single-handedly, but I also didn't want to leave him running around loose to kill more people. And I wanted to know why he did it. That was what he'd be counting on if he knew me. I had a chilling feeling that he *did* know me, and that firmed up my resolve. He could find me whenever he wanted to, and that gave me a distinctly uncomfortable feeling. The police had returned my gun. I checked it over carefully before replacing it in the holster under my arm and putting on my sports jacket and a plastic raincoat. The rain was beating steadily against the window and leaking in under the decayed sill. In a situation like this it was important not to be confused, and I wasn't. I wasn't doing this for the public or for Louise Madden or because I loved the Sydney Harbour Bridge. I was doing it for me.

My feet were wet before I reached the phone box, and I wondered how good a psychologist Lithgow was. Had he contrived to send me out in the cold and rain while he sat by a fire with one of his glasses of vintage red to hand? The lights from the traffic signals and the hotels and the car showrooms blurred in reflection on the wet road. The booth had lost a pane of glass to vandals, and the wind pushed spatters of rain inside, making the shelf and handset oily damp. The phone rang, and it almost slipped from my grasp as I snatched it up.

"Hardy."

"I want to explain."

"I understand."

"I wonder if you do. I wasn't fooled by the stories you planted in the papers."

Again, it seemed best not to say anything.

"I wasn't fooled for an instant," he went on. "It was very crude. But I admit I was hurt."

"Especially by references to your father."

His voice was almost a strangled sob. "What?"

"This is all to do with your father, isn't it?"

"Y-yes."

"What's your name?"

"Ballantine."

I'd read over the names of the injured many times. I hadn't retained them all, but Ballantine was the second name on the list. I couldn't go on not responding, and my mind raced to find something of sufficient weight to match what he'd revealed. Nothing came. "Ballantine," I said. "We were working on Goulburn or Bathurst."

"I told you I wasn't stupid. I want to talk with you."

"Okay. Where? When?"

"Where else?"

"On the bridge?"

"I'll meet you at the midpoint on the west side walkway. You come from the north. It'll take you about twenty minutes to get there. Come alone, Mr. Hardy, and don't try to trick me. I'll be watching you, and believe me I know every inch of the approaches and everything about the traffic flow at all times. Any sign that something is amiss will be immediately apparent to me. Do you understand?"

"Yes."

"I've given you my name, which makes me vulnerable to you. Almost as vulnerable as you are to me."

"I think you want help, Mr. Ballantine. I think you were asking me for it when you talked to me in the Pump Street house."

"Perhaps. I hope I can trust you."

I said, "You can," but not before he'd hung up. I hurried back to my car and drove across the bridge. I left the car down near the North Sydney swimming pool and jogged up to the walkway. The rain had stopped, and the sky had cleared; the wind was gusty, and the water far below was choppy. Traffic on the bridge was very light. Not much of a night for walking. As I moved toward the center of the bridge, I was aware that I had the north end of the walkway to myself. Ballantine knew his business: There were a few joggers on the east side, but foot passengers preferred the side away from the trains. A train rumbled past, and I saw a figure, caught in its headlight, approaching from the south side.

We met at about the middle of the span. Ballantine wore a short, padded coat with a fleecy collar turned up. His shoulders were hunched, and his head was dipped. It was hard to see his face, but his solid figure was unmistakable. He wore a cloth cap with a short peak. He nodded when we were within a few feet of each other and kept coming. "We'll walk across and back. This is going to take some time. Have you got a weapon?"

"No," I said.

"You're probably not telling the truth, but it doesn't matter. I've got an iron bar in my pocket here. I hope it stays there."

I turned, and we started to walk slowly back the way I'd come. "Whose idea was it to put those filthy stories in the papers?" Ballantine said.

His voice was low and controlled. I couldn't see any point in lying again. "A policeman named Meredith. He was investigating some of the disappearances: Samuels, Glover, and so on. He'd made the bridge connection, or almost, when I blundered in."

"A policeman, you say? I wouldn't have credited a policeman with the subtlety."

I felt I had to go on some sort of attack. "What happened with Glover? The body wasn't wrapped, and it broke free. That's when things started to fall into place."

"To answer that, I have to tell you how it all began. You see, I was brought up by my father, if you can call it an upbringing. I never knew my mother. She left when I was an infant. My father was crippled, in a wheelchair. He'd been severely wounded at Gallipoli and again in France. From the time I was about ten years old he was almost totally dependent on me. He couldn't work, but we had money. We lived in Drummoyne in a pleasant little house. Father told me he had inherited money, and he also had a service pension. Money wasn't a problem. I went to a good school."

We were walking slowly, barely moving, as if Ballantine were going to need hours to tell his story. I was cold, but I wasn't complaining. I was hearing the truth the way it's seldom told, painfully and with minute honesty.

"My father preached the military values ad nauseam. He said war was the true test of a man, the only real test. That women understood nothing and were worthless. I believed all these things. You do when you hear them from a man in a wheelchair who has ribbons and medals to back up what he says."

I nodded. Something about those words seemed immensely significant.

"I turned eighteen in 1944. I'd done cadet training at school and was keen to join up. Father wouldn't let me. He said he needed me to look after him. I pleaded with him, but he wouldn't relent. I tried to enlist under a false name, but they found me out. Father said he'd used his influence with the military authorities to stop me. I couldn't understand his attitude, and we had terrible fights over it. But he *did* need me. He seemed to get more frail by the day."

His voice was bitter now, and his shoulders were even more hunched. I wondered which pocket his iron bar was in.

"I tried to enlist for Korea. They rejected me on medical grounds. A burst eardrum, a heart murmur, they found a lot of things wrong with me. I suspected Father of fixing things again, and he didn't deny it. After that things got worse. He began to taunt me for not having served my country. Over and over again."

We got to the end of the path, and both automatically turned to walk back.

"I had a nervous breakdown. I was institutionalized for a time. Then I went back to take care of Father again, and so we went on, for years and years. It wasn't a real life. No friends, no women. While I was . . . in hospital, I learned to build boats. There were boatyards around Rozelle and Balmain in those days. I have great talent for it. I'm a very successful yacht builder and restorer. I have a small works in Drummoyne."

Never left home, I thought. *And what was it about that photograph of his father?*

"I don't want to bore you. I looked after Father until he died three years ago. He was in his late eighties, and he'd lived in a wheelchair for over sixty years. I hated him, but I couldn't help admiring his spirit. He was as nasty to me the day before he died as he had been the day the army rejected me. In a way, a sick way, I suppose, that was what kept us together. Anyway, he died, and I got used to being alone, and I continued to work. But after a time some questions began to occur to me. What about the service pension? I never got any correspondence about it. And when the numbers of Gallipoli survivors started to get down to a handful, I wondered why Father's name had never come up, why the journalists hadn't ever got on to him.

"I went into his room and dug out all the papers and things of his I'd never looked at, that he'd never let me look at. The only thing from his past he'd ever let me see was the photograph. The one you saw in my room in the Rocks."

"The ribbons!" I said.

Ballantine shook his head angrily. "Let me tell it. I dug through the papers and found that there never had been any inheritance. He'd won a lottery in 1934, bought the house, and invested the rest in other property. We lived well on the dividends all those years until my business brought in more than enough for us. But the worst thing was this: He'd never served in the army at all. Never!"

He was barely moving now and seemed unable to continue. I spoke softly, hoping to soothe him. "I was in the army. Did officer training and all that. We were supposed to know about the service ribbons, what they signified. Some of those ribbons in the photograph aren't Australian. It's been nagging at me ever since I saw the picture."

Ballantine nodded and began to speak quickly. "You're right. They're Canadian and New Zealand. It was all a fake, a fantasy. He worked on the bridge as a laborer from the late 1920s. He was injured in the fabrication workshop when a girder fell on him. He invented the war hero story, and I suffered because of it every day of my life. He was an evil man."

We were past the halfway point now, going south. I wondered how much longer the story would take and whether another crossing would be needed. Ballantine wasn't moving any more quickly, but the words were tumbling out.

"I met Barclay by accident. He came to me for some work on his boat. We talked. He told me about his father and the bridge. He was so pleased with himself in every way. His life had worked out so perfectly. His father had given him everything he'd ever wanted. And mine had taken everything away from me. I got into a rage, and I—I killed him. I couldn't believe that I'd done it at first, and then I couldn't believe how wonderful it made me feel. I tried to resist the impulse, but it was too strong for me. I searched out the others and killed them, too. I know it was wrong, but I couldn't help it."

"What about Glover?" I said.

"He was the worst. The most horrible person I ever met. The others weren't so bad, just so—so comfortable and self-satisfied. They were dead when I put them in the water, but Glover wasn't. I wanted him to be alive and aware of what was happening, so I didn't wrap him. It seems I didn't chain him properly either."

I didn't know what to do. He seemed calm, but there was a pent-up energy in him, and I knew how strong he was. He'd killed several fit, healthy men, and he said he had an iron bar in his pocket. I took a grip on the .38 in my pocket and plodded on.

"I got in touch with Stan Livermore as a way of finding the people I wanted. Old Stan knew everything about everyone connected with the bridge. I thought I might be able to help some of the veterans, too. But I didn't do anything for them. I'm sorry about old Stan. I didn't mean to kill him, just to frighten him so that he wouldn't say anything about me to you or anyone else. But I'd exhausted myself getting there before you, and there wasn't much time. I was a little panicked and too rough. He was very old and frail."

We were getting toward the south end of the bridge, and Ballantine suddenly sped up.

"I knew it was coming to an end. The feeling wasn't the same. The old woman was an awful creature, but I'm sorry about what happened to her."

I was almost trotting now to keep up with him. Suddenly he thrust his shoulder at me and sent me spinning, crashing into the metal barrier on my left. He swept my feet out from under me with a kick and broke into a run. I shouted and struggled up on a twisted ankle; I hobbled on, but he'd gained thirty feet on me. He stopped, and his arm swung up. I ducked, but he wasn't offering a threat. He was reaching up for something above him, something attached to the metal superstructure arching above us. Then he was climbing rapidly, hands and feet, clear of the walkway. A rope ladder. I limped forward, but before I could reach the spot, the ladder had been twitched up, up and away.

Ballantine climbed along a wide metal strut that intersected with a complex of girders and wires that reached up to a dizzying height. I stood rooted to the spot and watched him climb. He slid and slithered but clung on; he used his rope ladder to get over tricky parts, and he went up very high, very quickly. I got a look at the ladder; it was made of something light and slick, like nylon. A man came running toward me. "What're you doing?"

I pointed skyward. Ballantine had emerged from behind a pillar and was swarming up his ladder.

"Jesus," the man said, "should I get an ambulance or what?"

"You could use the emergency phone. Tell them there's a man climbing the bridge."

"Right." He dashed off, and I propped myself against the railing and stared up at the mass of gray metal. The man crawling and scrambling up it shrank to the size of a toy soldier. He was more than halfway to the top of the arch and still moving when I heard the sirens. They drew nearer, and the flashing lights started to lend a chaotic drama to the scene. The traffic slowed and snarled as drivers watched the crowd form. I was joined on the walkway by a policeman and other people who'd appeared from nowhere. A train roared along the tracks and drowned out the honking horns and screaming sirens. Unconsciously we shuffled back along the walkway toward the middle of the bridge, following the progress of the man above.

"My God," a woman said, "he's going to jump."

Ballantine reached a point where a strut ran out horizontally just below the center of the arch. He stood, balanced himself with both hands outstretched, and stepped out into the void. A whoosh of sound escaped the throats of the people watching as he plummeted. A fierce gust of wind twisted and turned him in the air and threw him against the railway overhead that jutted out beyond the arch not far above us. We heard the body hit with a soggy thump, and we gasped again as the impact flicked it back into space and it fell, fluttering and broken, into the dark water.

22

DAVID JOHN BALLANTINE, SIXTY-SIX, OF 21 BANKSIA STREET, DRUMMOYNE, HAD TOLD ME most of the truth about his life in our walk across the bridge. He'd omitted the fact that he'd been institutionalized several times for mental disorders. He had offered violence to himself and others over the years, but he was mostly in control and ran, as he'd said, a successful business as a boatbuilder and restorer. The police pieced his life together in the days after his battered body was taken from the harbor. They found ample evidence of his methods of killing and disposing of his victims. They found photographs and notes which showed how thoroughly he'd planned and executed the abductions and waylayings.

"The man got around Sydney using the waterways," Loomis told me. "He must've known the harbor like the back of his hand. And he was immensely strong. He killed those men with his bare hands, quickly and efficiently. He actually threw one of them over a high fence and into some bushes as a temporary hiding place. Handling them was no problem."

"Tell me, when they fished him out, did he have an iron bar in his pocket?"

"No. Funny thing was, he had a bunch of military medals and ribbons, all crammed together in the pocket of his coat."

"He'd have done better to have snuffed his father early on," I said.

Loomis nodded. "The father must have been a monster, but make no mistake, Ballantine was very strange himself. Paranoid to an immense degree. He really thought the whole world was out to screw him. Beautiful craftsman, though. You should see some of the model boats he made. Beautiful."

"Did you find his boat?"

"Sort of. He'd holed and sunk it in the water near his slipway. They tell me it was a butcher's boat. Appropriate, eh?"

"A butcher's boat," I said. "What's that?"

"Apparently the butchers used to race each other out to the ships in the old days. First aboard got the provisioning order. They had these light, fast boats. Lithgow had restored his down to the last nail. Ideal for dumping bodies. He was saying good-bye when he sank it, poor bastard."

"How's Lloyd Meredith?"

"Mending. We would have got Ballantine ourselves, Hardy. You realize that."

"Sure," I said. "While on the subject of getting people, what about Tobin?"

"Conspiracy to commit murder, attempted murder, he's going inside for a long, long time."

"Good," I said. "Moody?"

"Resigned. Pissed off about something or other. It's not a perfect world, Hardy."

Louise Madden buried her father in the cemetery at Blackheath in the Blue Mountains. I drove up there for the occasion. It was a fine, cold day in the mountains, and there were a lot of people present: Brian Madden's former colleagues, some of his ex-students, a number of Louise's friends, people from the golf club. I looked around for Dell Burton, the other woman who grieved for Madden, but she wasn't there. We all stood in the small space available between other graves and watched the quiet, dignified ceremony. Louise held the handful of earth a long time before dropping it in on the box.

Later, back at her rambling weatherboard house in Leura, she thanked me for giving her the chance to say good-bye to her father properly.

I sipped my drink and didn't say anything.

She was almost smiling. "Cheer up, it means

a lot to me, all this. Having people around. Do *any* of your cases have a really happy ending, Cliff?"

"Not lately," I said. "But I keep hoping."

Robert B. PARKER

"The toughest, funniest, wisest private-eye in the field."*

☐ A CATSKILL EAGLE	11132-3	$4.99
☐ CEREMONY	10993-0	$4.99
☐ CRIMSON JOY	20343-0	$4.99
☐ EARLY AUTUMN	12214-7	$5.99
☐ GOD SAVE THE CHILD	12899-4	$5.99
☐ THE GODWULF MANUSCRIPT	12961-3	$5.99
☐ THE JUDAS GOAT	14196-6	$4.99
☐ LOOKING FOR RACHEL WALLACE	15316-6	$4.99
☐ LOVE AND GLORY	14629-1	$4.99
☐ MORTAL STAKES	15758-7	$5.99
☐ PROMISED LAND	17197-0	$4.99
☐ A SAVAGE PLACE	18095-3	$5.99
☐ TAMING A SEAHORSE	18841-5	$4.99
☐ VALEDICTION	19246-3	$5.99
☐ THE WIDENING GYRE	19535-7	$4.99
☐ WILDERNESS	19328-1	$4.99

The Houston Post

Match wits with the best-selling

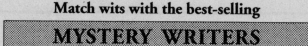

MYSTERY WRITERS

in the business!

SUSAN DUNLAP

"Dunlap's police procedurals have the authenticity of telling detail."
—*The Washington Post Book World*

☐	**AS A FAVOR**	20999-4	$3.99
☐	**ROGUE WAVE**	21197-2	$4.99
☐	**DEATH AND TAXES**	21406-8	$4.99
☐	**KARMA**	20982-X	$3.99
☐	**A DINNER TO DIE FOR**	20495-X	$4.99
☐	**DIAMOND IN THE BUFF**	20788-6	$4.99
☐	**NOT EXACTLY A BRAHMIN**	20998-6	$4.99
☐	**TIME EXPIRED**	21683-4	$4.99
☐	**TOO CLOSE TO THE EDGE**	20356-2	$4.99
☐	**PIOUS DECEPTION**	20746-0	$3.99

SARA PARETSKY

"Paretsky's name always makes the top of the list when people talk about the new female operatives." —*The New York Times Book Review*

☐	**BLOOD SHOT**	20420-8	$5.99
☐	**BURN MARKS**	20845-9	$5.99
☐	**INDEMNITY ONLY**	21069-0	$5.99
☐	**GUARDIAN ANGEL**	21399-1	$5.99
☐	**KILLING ORDERS**	21528-5	$5.99

SISTER CAROL ANNE O'MARIE

"Move over Miss Marple..." —*San Francisco Sunday Examiner & Chronicle*

☐	**ADVENT OF DYING**	10052-6	$3.99
☐	**THE MISSING MADONNA**	20473-9	$4.99
☐	**A NOVENA FOR MURDER**	16469-9	$3.99
☐	**MURDER IN ORDINARY TIME**	21353-3	$4.99
☐	**MURDER MAKES A PILGRIMAGE**	21613-3	$4.99

LINDA BARNES

☐	**COYOTE**	21089-5	$4.99
☐	**STEEL GUITAR**	21268-5	$4.99
☐	**SNAPSHOT**	21220-0	$4.99
☐	**BITTER FINISH**	21606-0	$4.99

At your local bookstore or use this handy page for ordering:

DELL READERS SERVICE, DEPT. DS
2451 South Wolf Rd., Des Plaines, IL. 60018

Please send me the above title(s). I am enclosing $ _____
(Please add $2.50 per order to cover shipping and handling.) Send check or money order—no cash or C.O.D.s please.

Dell

Ms./Mrs./Mr. _____

Address _____

City/State _____ Zip _____

DGM-1/95

Prices and availability subject to change without notice. Please allow four to six weeks for delivery.